THE NITTY-GRITTY OF MONEY

CONSTRUCTING 12 MONEY PRINCIPLES FOR YOUTH AND ADULTS.

BRAD BRUNKOW

WESTBOW·
PRESS
A DIVISION OF THOMAS NELSON
& ZONDERVAN

This is a work of fiction. All of the characters, names, incidents, organizations, and dialogue in this novel are either the products of the author's imagination or are used fictitiously.

WestBow Press books may be ordered through booksellers or by contacting:

WestBow Press
A Division of Thomas Nelson & Zondervan
1663 Liberty Drive
Bloomington, IN 47403
www.westbowpress.com
1 (866) 928-1240

Because of the dynamic nature of the Internet, any web addresses or links contained in this book may have changed since publication and may no longer be valid. The views expressed in this work are solely those of the author and do not necessarily reflect the views of the publisher, and the publisher hereby disclaims any responsibility for them.

ISBN: 978-1-4908-7633-7 (sc)
ISBN: 978-1-4908-7632-0 (hc)
ISBN: 978-1-4908-7631-3 (e)

Library of Congress Control Number: 2015905691

Print information available on the last page.

WestBow Press rev. date: 5/1/2015

Contents

This book is dedicated to you. This book is to service you as a grandparent, parent, son, or daughter who is an adult or youth to grow in your Christian faith as you manage your money. This book presents through a story twelve Christian-based fundamental, lifelong money principles. I hope that this story sparks an interest not only in learning, but also in practicing a Christian approach to money management. Best wishes to you and enjoy the following pages.

Foreword

As a citizen of a country careening toward a $20-trillion national debt, I'd say money management is an important topic not only for CHRISTians but for all people. Brad Brunkow, a lifelong, committed Lutheran CHRISTian, has written a little book that will make a big impact. The wisdom imparted in this book is practiced in the lives of Brad and his family. I can attest to that from personal knowledge.

C'mon along and meet Grandpa, Grandma, Ryan, and Kayla. Grandpa and Grandma put Ryan and Kayla through what might be described as "Money Management Boot Camp," as they lovingly and patiently urge and challenge their grandchildren to adopt the timeless money management principles of the Bible.

This book is fun. It is educational. It is relational. (The loving patience of Grandpa and Grandma is clearly modeled after our heavenly Father.) It is encouraging. It is thought provoking. And it will make a big impact on the way you think about the gift of God that is money, even if you think you "know it all" already.

Tom Ramsey
Pastor Emeritus

Preface

The needs of our present-day culture are complex and numerous. Seeing a need and then doing something about it as a reflection of our love for our Savior, Jesus Christ, is basic to a life lived as a Christian. I have observed a need for families and individuals to be better money managers. Managing personal finance is a complex task, and the earlier a person learns and practices basic principles about money, the better a money manager that person will be.

The purpose of this book is to present a complete set of basic principles to manage money in daily life as a Christian. The goal was to make it readable to students in grades 5 through 8; however, the principles apply to all age groups, up to and including adults. The book was written from a Christian perspective. Without a Christian perspective, you will obtain money concepts, but not have a holistic perspective for them. One way to read this book is to read a chapter aloud as part of family time over a couple of weeks. Some of the later chapters cover topics that a grade school student may have difficulty grasping. These chapters in particular would be helpful to read in conjunction with family discussions. The harder concepts may not be understood until students are older, but better they be introduced to them too soon rather than too late. Also, I believe it is important to present a relatively complete set of principles rather than a partial set. Keep the book and refer back to these topics with students when the time is right.

As a suggestion, make up some of your own games and activities to increase students' understanding of managing money. Or try doing the same activities as the children in this story.

The characters are fictional, but hopefully realistic enough to provide a tangible way of learning about and discussing basic money principles with the family.

All scripture quotations are taken from the Holy Bible, New International Version®, NIV® Copyright © 1973, 1978, 1984, 2011 by International Bible Society.

I wish to acknowledge Reverend Tom Ramsey, who has been a very positive influence on my Christian faith in Jesus, our Lord and Savior, and my application of faith in my daily life. Much of Reverend Ramsey's Biblical teaching and preaching regarding money is woven into this book.

I also wish to acknowledge Jacob Colle, who created the illustrations and the cover. He is a young Christian man who also is utilizing his talent to show his love for his Savior.

I also thank my family, especially my wife, Susan, who provided input, support, and life experience about these topics.

Best wishes to you. I hope this book helps you in your walk through this life on earth.

CHAPTER 1

The First Step Is Challenging

School was out for the summer. Ryan and Kayla had a huge list of fun things they were planning to do. They planned to swim, camp, hike, go on vacation, and do everything else they could cram in before school restarted. They were also looking forward to spending a few weeks with their grandparents. Compared to their mom and dad, their grandparents seemed to have more time to do fun things.

Ryan and Kayla counted their money as they planned their trip to Grandpa and Grandma's. They planned to take some cash along to add to the fun of their stay. Their dad popped in and said, "This year your visit to Grandpa and Grandma is going to be exciting! They are planning a money camp where you will learn and earn some money while you are there. So you can leave your money at home this time."

Ryan quickly had thoughts about a money hunt and finding bags full of money. Kayla had a vision of a magical money tree with leaves made of dollar bills. They started putting away their money and talked about changes with some of their friends. Some had moved away because of job changes in their families. Two houses in their neighborhood had been taken back by the banks. They heard frequent conversations about money problems and the tensions that created in some families.

1

After a week of anticipation, it was time to visit their grandparents. The trip was a few hours' travel to the medium-sized city where their grandparents lived. Mom and Dad stayed to have ham sandwiches and visit for a few hours, and then they left for home. The kids and their grandparents played darts, went for a walk, and later, got ready for bed.

As they were doing their final nighttime chores, Grandpa said, "Tomorrow we will start our journey of learning about money." Wow—that was all it took for Ryan and Kayla to think about all the great things they could get with more money. They said their prayers to finish the night but had trouble falling asleep, much like at Christmastime, as they were thinking about the mysterious events of the coming days.

The next morning was a beautiful day. The birds were singing, there was a pleasant, cool breeze, and plenty of flowers were in bloom. "After breakfast, as soon as you are ready, we will take our first money trip," Grandma said. In half the time it took them to get ready for school, Ryan and Kayla were ready and were waiting at the door.

"I will give each of you $2 if either of you can guess where we are going," Grandpa said. "But you cannot start guessing until we are on the road, and you have only six tries."

When they were on the road, Ryan yelled, "A bank!"

"Nope, sorry," Grandma said.

Kayla saw a library. "A library," she blurted out.

"Sorry, that is not it," said Grandpa.

Kayla spotted a loan company. "A loan company?" she asked hesitantly.

"Wrong again," said Grandma.

They went by a small college. "Are you taking us to a school?" asked Ryan.

"Nope," said Grandpa.

Kayla and Ryan both spotted a sign that said "Money Markets, Securities, Brokers, and Advisors." "Are we going to that money place over there that says something about brokers and advisors on it?" asked Kayla.

"Those are all good guesses, but that is still not it," Grandpa answered.

About that time, they pulled into the church parking lot. "Church?" Ryan asked.

"Is church your final guess?" Grandma replied.

Ryan and Kayla whispered to each other that they could not think of anything else. "We are out of ideas, so yes, church is our last guess," Kayla answered.

"Right you are. Church it is, and you each win $2," Grandpa said.

The children felt a mix of emotions. They were happy to get a few dollars, but totally confused about why their first lesson about money was at church. They had thought this was going to be fun, but now it seemed more serious. Would it still be fun? Would they still learn about money?

Grandpa said, "'The fear of the LORD is the beginning of knowledge, but fools despise wisdom and instruction.' That is what Proverbs 1:7 says. You see, God created everything, and he desires to be a part of everything we have and do. God wants to be first in our lives. If money is first, we will never have enough. As humans, we always want more. Putting God first does not mean you will necessarily have more money. But you will have more of what God really wants for you to have. He really wants us to have the fruit of the Spirit, as it says in Galatians 5:22–23: 'But the fruit of the Spirit is love, joy, peace, forbearance, kindness, goodness, faithfulness, gentleness and self-control. Against such things there is no law.' A more common word for forbearance is patience."

Grandma also explained that to fear the Lord is to respect and trust God, to put him first in our lives. She listed the fruit of the Spirit and talked about each one. She had many pieces of advice. "Money may be able to buy some earthly security, but it cannot buy love. Money may bring some short-term happiness, but it cannot buy joy. Money may be able to buy some comfort, but it cannot buy peace. Money may be able to buy some time-saving devices, but it cannot buy patience. Money may enable a person to do nice things for others, but it cannot buy kindness. Money by itself is not good or bad; goodness is what comes from the heart as a reflection of our love for Jesus."

Grandma continued, "Faith is trusting God's promises. Money can be a barricade that gets in the way of our faith. Gentleness is strength under control. Money can be a resource of strength to get our desires. It is important to have our strength under control and in alignment with God's wishes so that we control ourselves and treat ourselves and others gently. Self-control is managing ourselves in a God-pleasing way. Money can all too easily become our god and control us, rather than us controlling our money. Money certainly cannot buy self-control."

Ryan stated, "This is just too complicated already. If this is lesson one about money, I am never going to figure this out."

"You are right, Ryan," Grandma replied. "It is complicated. But God has an easy plan for us to follow in regards to our money. When we earn some money, God desires us to bring him a tithe, which is 10 percent of what we earn, to express our love and respect for him. It is a simple target. In terms of money, doing his will is putting him first. Malachi 3:10 says, "'Bring the whole tithe into the storehouse, that there may be food in my house. Test me in this," says the LORD Almighty, "and see if I will not throw open the floodgates of heaven and pour out so much blessing that there will not be room enough to store it.'" In simple terms, God is telling us to remember him with our first earnings and he will take care of us. If we do his will, we will be on the road to receiving the things that really matter. The blessings that really matter are fruit of the Spirit, and they cannot be bought with money. Recall that the fruit of the Spirit is love, joy, peace, patience, kindness, goodness, faithfulness, gentleness, and self-control."

"So, since we each earned $2 for guessing the location of our first lesson, I think we should each give 10 percent, or 20 cents, to church or Sunday school to show our respect and love for God," Kayla said.

"Exactly," Grandma replied. "Do first what God desires of you, and the rest of your life will start to work the way it should. If we ignore this important first step, who knows what crazy things that could have been avoided may come our way? Because God loved us first, he wants us to demonstrate our love for him. In regards to money, a tithe is a good target. Offerings are additional gifts of love over and above a tithe. You can study 1 Corinthians 16:1–4 and 2 Corinthians 8–9 sometime to learn more about New Testament giving. These verses teach that giving should be from our love for Jesus. Giving should be regular and proportional to what we earn. As your faith grows, your giving will grow, too. But for now, let's keep it simple and target a tithe or 10 percent of what you earn."

> With all things, put God first. A tithe (10 percent) is a good benchmark for putting God first with our money.

"Here is one last Bible verse," said Grandpa. "Second Corinthians 9:7 says, 'Each of you should give what you have decided in your heart to give, not reluctantly or under compulsion, for God loves a cheerful giver.' Now let's go play in the park and then head home for cookies and a board game."

After saying the Lord's Prayer that evening, Ryan and Kayla shared a conversation. "You know, being a child is fun," Kayla said. "You do not have to worry much and you get to have a ton of fun. Maybe if we put God first, like we learned today, we can be children for life—God's children. Putting him first by doing the simple act of tithing opens the door to remaining his children. It looks like that can be part of our plan to be in his hands forever."

"That seems to make sense," said Ryan, "but it must be more complicated. I remember my schoolteacher saying the hardest step is the first step. So this first step of tithing may be a challenge. I will have to practice it. I think the teacher also said that the first step, no matter how small or large it is, needs to be in the right direction. It points us in the direction we want to go. Step the wrong way, and you will end up in the wrong place. Maybe that is what Grandma meant about regular and proportional giving. If someone cannot cheerfully give a tithe right away, maybe they can start a regular and proportional gift and then work their way up to a tithe or more."

"Tithing is like pouring a foundation for a house. It is the first thing to do and you want to do it right," said Kayla.

"Yes," replied Ryan. "It feels like we have constructed our first money lesson."

They fell asleep, not as excited as they had been the first night, but certainly at peace, knowing they were part of a loving family, and in wonder of the might of God, who created us and the world we live in.

CHAPTER 2

Money and Means

The next morning, the kids woke up and smelled bacon cooking. "Hooray! Bacon with breakfast!" Kayla yelled as she ran off to see what else there was to eat.

At the morning feast, Ryan asked Grandpa, "I have a question about expressing our love and respect for God with our money. We are to give 10 percent of what we earn for the work of the church. What happens if someone gives me birthday money? I did not earn that, but do I still give God 10 percent of it?"

Grandpa explained. "If you get a gift from us, you can rest assured that we gave a tithe or more before giving you your gift. It is a gift from us and an expression of our love for you. You did not earn the money, so I think you can do with it as you please, since it was a gift to you. You might be moved to give a portion as an offering or tithe—that would be your choice. If we gave you an object rather than money, could you carve off 10 percent of it as an offering for God? That would be rather difficult. But you might be able to use that gift in ways that are pleasing to God. We certainly should not use a gift in a way that is displeasing to God. Remember, all giving is in response to the greatest gift, eternal life, which we receive through Jesus. Breakfast today is another example. Breakfast was also a gift to you, but how can you give a portion of your breakfast as a tithe? The breakfast was for you to enjoy, much like your birthday money. But we did stop to honor God and say a prayer of thanksgiving to him before we ate. I am sure he appreciated that. It might be a good idea to thank Grandma, also. You can talk more with your mom and dad about giving from gifts you receive."

"So where are we going today?" Kayla asked. "Back to church to learn more about God and our Savior, Jesus?"

"This time, we are going to school," Grandma replied.

"Do we bring our calculators?" Ryan asked with a puzzled expression.

"No, just bring an open mind," said Grandpa.

The last thing the kids wanted to do was go to school. After all, it was summer. They took a long time to get ready and required some encouragement to stay on schedule. Finally, they all got in the car and went on their way—the kids were less than excited. They pulled into the parking lot of the local college.

"College? We're not ready for college," Kayla said.

"I think you already understand lesson two," Grandma responded.

"What? I do not get it," said Ryan.

They walked around some of the large buildings and found a shady place with some benches. The yard was freshly mown and the smell of cut grass filled the air. They also heard noisy crickets that sounded like they were upset the grass had been cut.

"You said you were not ready for college. Tell me some reasons you think you are not ready," Grandma said.

The kids rattled off several reasons:

- They needed to complete more grades first.
- They would not be able to understand the classes.

- They would not know how to find all their classes in such a big place.
- They wanted to be kids for longer.
- They had not yet started learning higher math.
- They could not drive, like these big kids could.
- They did not want to miss the special class trip coming up next year.

"So, are you saying you have to be like a boy scout, that you have to be prepared first in order to be ready for college?" Grandma asked.

"Yes, that is right. You cannot just jump ahead in school and expect it to work out," said Ryan.

"Money is just like that," said Grandma. "You must live within your means. In other words, you must make do with the money you have and manage it well. Just like you have to learn and grow before going to the next grade in school, you have to learn and grow in your skills with money. You both have some money now. If you spend it all now, but then next week, something comes along that you wish you had the money for, you may be tempted to ask for a loan or an advance from your mom and dad. A loan, or borrowing money, is like skipping ahead in school. When you get a loan, you are obtaining more money than you have demonstrated that you can manage. Remember the fruit of the Spirit? One was self-control. Self-control helps you control your desires so that they fit into the resources, or money, that you have. You may still have larger desires than you have money to fulfill, but you will have the patience to contently live without those things or wait until you are ready or able to have them."

"Some friends of mine seem to get everything they want. Their parents buy them everything," said Kayla.

"That does not teach your friends very much about living within their means," said Grandma. "Getting everything they want is nice for now, but they are not learning much about self-control or managing their money. Knowing the difference between wants and needs is key to living within your means. We are going to pack a lunch and wade in the creek by the cool spring today. How about we give each of you $1, and you can pick out any candy you want for dessert? You can live within your means by purchasing any candy you want as long as it is no more than $1."

"So we do not have to go to school after all?" asked Ryan.

Grandma replied, "We did go to school, but we are almost done with it today. We learned that, just as in school, we move up from grade to grade, we need to learn to live within our means and move up within the limits of our money. Here is a useful Bible verse: Hebrews 13:5 says, 'Keep your lives free from the love of money and be content with what you have, because God has said, "Never will I leave you; never will I forsake you."' Here is another: 1 Timothy 6:10 says, 'For the love of money is a root of all kinds of evil. Some people, eager for money, have wandered from the faith and pierced themselves with many griefs.' These verses tell us again to put God first and live within our means. Money by itself is not evil; it is the love of money that is evil. This does not mean you lack ambition. It means you pace yourself through life like you pace yourself through school, learning and doing what you are capable of now so that you can be more capable in the future. If you practice living within your means, you will also learn how to save some of your money and not spend it all. This saving will be used later in life for your needs or wants."

> Be content: Know the difference between wants and needs.
>
> - Live within your means.
> - Avoid debt in daily living.
> - Practice saving.

"I get it. I think I know how to remember this," said Kayla. "Some teachers are mean—well, I know they care about us. But they do make us stay within the rules to help us learn, and in that way, they may seem mean. Really, they are helping us grow up at the level where we are so that someday, we can manage high school and more."

"I think you've got it. Let's go get some candy bars, pack a lunch, and head to the spring," Grandpa replied.

"I want something with peanut butter," Kayla said with excitement.

They enjoyed lunch and the rest of the afternoon. The kids did not think wading was going to be that much fun, but the water was cool, they found a large water boatman bug, they built a few dams in the water, and they really had a great time. The fun was free, which certainly was within their means.

That night, brother and sister chitchatted in the dark before falling asleep. "You know, it was nice to have the candy bar for a snack, but I really had a pretty good time playing in the water," said Kayla, contemplating. "And we did not spend any money to have the fun. I did not know Grandpa had that powerful squirt gun that he ambushed us with. Inside, he must be a little kid, too."

"Yep, I agree, "said Ryan. "I want one of those squirt guns, too. I was thinking about what you said about the lesson on tithing. You said tithing is like pouring the foundation first. I guess this lesson was kind of like trying to put a roof on a house before the walls have been completed. That would be silly."

"That would be silly," Kayla agreed. "Good night."

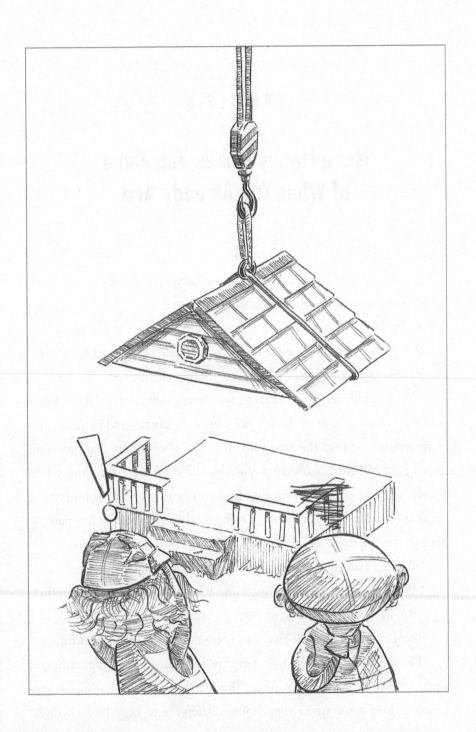

CHAPTER 3

More Money Makes You More of What You Already Are

There was no smell of bacon the next morning. The sound of cereal boxes, bowls, and spoons woke the children.

At breakfast, Kayla asked, "So, if someone takes out loans to get the things they want for every day, then money will start to control their life—is that right?"

"Yes," said Grandpa. "Having too much debt or too many loans is like a modern form of slavery. You become controlled by debts and obligations and lose the freedom to make choices or changes. You may be forced to make loan payments at a difficult time, like when something unexpected comes up that you must pay for. You may not be able to make the payments. Living within our means is a path to long-term freedom of choice and avoiding unnecessary loans."

"Well, what are we learning today?" asked Ryan.

"We are going to drive around and look at houses," said Grandma.

"We are going to learn about real estate?" asked Kayla.

"Not really. You will find out soon enough," said Grandma.

They drove around some neighborhoods and saw apartments, then rental houses, then what their grandparents called starter houses, then some quite nice houses, then some very large houses, and a few really giant houses that looked like mansions. They discussed what they liked about each house and the kinds of flowers and trees they saw.

"So, what is the point of this?" asked Ryan.

Grandpa responded, "Think back to the kinds of houses we looked at. Who do you think has the most money?"

"The people in the really big houses!" Ryan said with certainty.

"Not necessarily," said Grandpa. "Certainly those with larger houses very likely have larger incomes, but they don't necessarily have more money. They may be in debt or have taken such large loans to buy their houses that they have no more money in their possession than the people with smaller houses. Those with very large loans may be spending all their income. Think back to yesterday, when we gave you $1 for candy. What would you have done if we had given you $2 for a candy bar?"

"I would have bought two candy bars," Ryan said, grinning.

"You are a hungry boy," Grandma chuckled. "And that is how the typical person manages their money. The more they get, the more they spend. Typically, a rise in income is matched by a rise in spending."

"More money just makes you more of what you already are," said Grandma. "You want to be wise with a little, so that later, if you have more, you will be wise with more. If you are greedy with a little, you will likely be greedy with a lot. If you spend it all when you have a small amount, you will likely spend it all when you have a large amount. To increase your financial wealth or financial freedom, your growth in spending should not exceed your growth in income. There is nothing wrong with having a nice house or a nice big house. However, if that comes at the cost of financial freedom, leaving no cushion for the future, it could be a stressful situation."

Grandpa added, "Wealth is the accumulation of money that can be used to support your living, to be helpful to others, or to give you the freedom to make more choices. I read the other day that many people do not accumulate much wealth because they buy houses that are too expensive or cars that are too fancy for their means. If you take out a loan, you will pay much more in total—because of interest—than if you save the money beforehand. A loan for a house is not bad. It is great to have a place of your own that you can call home and a house should have lasting value. It is a concern if a house loan consumes too much of your income. The previous lesson we were concerned about loans for everyday things, and things that do not last."

> More money just makes you more of what you already are, so learn and practice your money values early on.

"To learn about accumulating more money, do we get $2 for candy today, and we can spend $1 but keep $1 for later?" asked Kayla.

"You kids sure think fast," Grandma replied. "How about today we make some candy? We can use the items I have at home. More money in the future is not a sure thing, so let us use what we have at home for now. Even though we are not going to buy any candy, we have options. Our option today is to make our own candy. We can be just as happy and enjoy some freedom from spending money. Ecclesiastes 5:10 says, 'Whoever loves money never has enough; whoever loves wealth is never satisfied with their income. This too is meaningless.'"

"Sounds good to me. I like those peanut butter balls you make. Can we make those?" asked Ryan.

"Sure we can do that, and some other candy you guys like. We will also make extra for you to take home to your mom and dad," said Grandma, rolling her tongue around her lips like she was licking off icing.

They spent a large part of the day making candy, licking bowls, getting sticky, and playing games. They learned a lot about proportions, temperature, following recipes, staying clean, using kitchen gadgets, and even working together. They enjoyed some of their hard work as dessert, too.

That evening, they had devotion and read the parable of the talents, also called the parable of the bags of gold, in Matthew 25:14–30. They discussed how this parable told by Jesus illustrated how each servant managed the affairs of the master and how each was expected to manage appropriately, even though they had been given responsibility of different amounts. Even the manager who was given the least was expected to act within his capability or, at the very least, to hire someone else to manage the money for him, like by putting it in the bank. The parable was not just about money, but also about our skills and talents. We should try to do well and be good in all categories of life.

As the kids were brushing their teeth that night, Kayla noticed a multitude of tiny white dots on the mirror. "What is that?" asked Kayla.

"I don't know," said Ryan as he kept brushing. But more dots appeared.

"Ryan, those dots are flinging off your toothbrush. Some of that spray just hit me in the face! You need to keep your mouth closed. We are messing up Grandma's bathroom! We need to be more careful, like we learned in that parable!" Kayla yelped. They both got the giggles and started making faces at each other, using their toothpaste and toothbrushes to help create even more far-out expressions.

That night after prayers, the kids had a discussion about money. "So how do you think Grandpa and Grandma manage their money?" asked Kayla.

Ryan responded, "I think they must have followed the lessons they are teaching us. They seem to be very happy. They obviously love and respect God. They frequently thank Jesus for forgiveness of sins, for family, and for the life they have. They seem to have all the money they want—certainly all they need. They sure are generous with us. I'm enjoying spending some time getting to know them a little better."

"I agree," Kayla said. "Good night and see you in the morning."

CHAPTER 4

Choices and Priorities Are a Budget

The next morning, the kids woke up before their grandparents. They decided it was time for them to serve, so they got out the breakfast items and waited quietly for their grandparents to get up.

"Well, isn't this a surprise!" exclaimed Grandma. "Thank you very much. This is nice."

"We got to thinking, if more money makes you more of what you already are, then we should practice being nice," said Ryan. "That way, we will get more money sooner, rather than later," he joked.

"So, what is the plan for today?" asked Kayla.

"Today we learn about choices," Grandpa said.

"That's easy," said Kayla. "I want to do everything!"

"That is a common problem with money," Grandpa said. "People want to do everything, not realizing they must make choices and set priorities over what they wish to do."

"Priorities? Can you explain priorities?" Ryan asked.

Grandpa responded, "Setting priorities is listing what is important, from most to least important. The items of least importance, which are at the bottom of the list, may never happen. Think back to our first lesson. If God is at the top of our list and we make him a part of what we are doing, he will not fall off our list. That does not mean we must go to church every day, but it does mean that the things we do should be things that God can be part of. Today we plan to have fun and learn about priorities and choices. We will give each of you a $20 budget to plan to spend on activities for the day. I will give you a list to choose from. When you review the list, you will see that we cannot do everything, but we can certainly do a lot. The rules will go like this: One, we all go together. Two, we need to be home by 10:00 p.m. Three, you each have $20 maximum to spend. Four, we cannot skip meals. And finally, five, I have to approve any activity you add to this list. On the list are the prices per person and the times for the activities. Here it is: start planning your budget of time and money for today."

Ryan and Kayla excitedly studied the list that Grandpa gave them.

Lunch at grandparents'	$1	Time required: 1 hour
Supper at grandparents'	$2	Time required: 1 hour
Nap	Free	
Play in park	Free	
Water park—all day	$18	
Water park—after 6:00 pm	$10	Open to 9:00 p.m.
Lunch at water park	$6	
Lunch—fast food	$5	
Supper—fast food	$5	
Supper at water park	$6	
Movie at 1:00	$5	Time required: 3 hours
Movie after 5:00	$8	Time required: 3 hours
Movie rental	$2	Time required: 2 hours
Mini golf round	$3	Time required: 1 hour
Ice cream snack	$2	Time required: 30 minutes
Arcade place	$6	Time required: 2 hours

"So, what is the weather supposed to be like?" asked Ryan.

"Fairly hot and sunny all day," Grandpa responded.

The kids had a serious conference. The one choice they quickly decided to scratch was a nap. That was the lowest priority. They decided a nap would only be priority if they were paid to have it. They really wanted to go to the water park, but if they did that all day, they would only get to do one thing, and also, they did not have enough money to eat two meals there, so it would not work. After quite a lot of deliberation, this is what they presented.

Morning:	Play in the park	$0
Lunch:	Pack lunch at park	$1
Afternoon:	Movie at 1:00	$5
Supper:	At home	$2
Evening:	Water park 6:00–9:00	$10
	Ice cream snack	$2
Total		$20 (each)

"You sure have learned how to spend every penny," laughed Grandpa. "I am really proud of you. You filled an entire day with activities and learned how to make choices and set some priorities. I think you know what a budget is about. Yes, a packed lunch counts the same as eating at home. Do you want to head to the park in about thirty minutes, after we pack the lunch?"

"Sure thing," the kids replied.

The grandparents plotted their own day as they packed the lunches. They decided they would go to the park with the kids, then come home and take a nap and then fix supper while the kids were at the movies. After supper, they would go along to the water park to watch the kids play in the water and join them for the ice cream dessert. They agreed it would be a fun day for them, too.

The budget for the day went just as planned. Other than a skinned knee and stubbed toe from the water slide, everyone had a great time. While they were eating their ice cream, they started to reflect on the day.

"This lesson on spending money was sure a lot of fun. It is fun spending money," said Ryan.

"Yes, it is fun to spend money," Grandma replied. "If we had given each of you $40 to spend, instead of $20, would you have had twice as much fun?"

"I do not think so," said Kayla. "I think the day was just fine because we learned how to budget our money and time and we still got to ride the largest water slide seven times! Twenty dollars was enough and the idea of making choices helped us plan a fun day. The day was full enough. I think I am ready for that free nap now. I have heard our parents talk about their budget and how it helps them prioritize and make choices. Is that what we did today?"

Grandpa replied, "Yes, you learned how to make some choices and prioritize your money and time. Those are the basics of a budget. If you can budget with a little, you should also be able to budget with more. Today it was fine to spend all the budget; that was the plan. But you will discover that it is not always best to spend it all. Have you heard of the word frugal? Being frugal means spending your money wisely and also fairly. Wisely means you understand how much you have to spend on those things that you need or want. When you understand your situation, you look and wait for the right time and price. Being fair means you do not cheat others in that process. I think today you were also frugal with your budget."

> Budgeting is setting and following priorities and choices about money and time.

They finished their ice cream and arrived home at about 9:45, just within the plan. They had a short devotion and read a couple of Bible passages.

> The plans of the diligent lead to profit as surely as haste leads to poverty.
>
> —Proverbs 21:5

Grandma explained that being diligent is working in a persistent and careful way. Being persistent means you keep working at something for a long time, even if it is hard. They talked about how a budget is a diligent plan for money.

> Be sure you know the condition of your flocks, give careful attention to your herds; for riches do not endure forever, and a crown is not secure for all generations.
>
> —Proverbs 27:23–24

They talked about how having a budget is a good plan for being diligent with your money. They also decided that following the plan and tracking its progress is important for managing into the future.

Ryan and Kayla were tired and they slithered off to bed. No additional white toothpaste specks showed up on the mirror this time. They each reflected to themselves about how planning their day really had worked quite well, and how, at first, the $20 had not seemed like a lot. They were proud to have figured out how to do not everything, but enough to still be content and happy, and to have learned about budgeting at the same time. The idea of a budget seemed to be a good one.

After they said prayers they quickly fell asleep.

CHAPTER 5

Demand and Supply

The kids slept thirty minutes past their normal breakfast time the next morning. The long night had helped them recover from their previous big day. Sleepily, they walked into the kitchen for breakfast.

"Good morning, sleepyheads. I already have your breakfast ready for you," said Grandma.

"Where is it?" asked Ryan. "All I see is a few crackers and a tiny glass of juice."

"That's it. You found it," Grandma replied.

"This is strange. Are we learning to be penny pinchers, or homeless, or about fasting?" asked Kayla.

"No, but throughout your life, you will find that the things you remember vividly will have actions and feelings associated with them. So this is a meal you likely will never forget," Grandma stated.

"You are right about that," said Ryan. "My stomach is not going to let me forget this breakfast."

"This is part of the lesson for today," Grandpa said. "Our topic today is more abstract. Abstract means not as easy to understand. It is a topic you may not hear much about until you are in a college-level class. But it is common sense, so you will understand, especially with your stomach talking to you."

"I think my stomach is already growling with demand. I hope lunch is around 10:00 a.m. today!" exclaimed Ryan.

"Demand—that is part of the lesson today," Grandpa said, smiling.

"How about you get ready, and then we will go to the grocery store?" Grandma said.

"Grocery store? That will be torture after a breakfast like this," said Ryan.

"You will live, I assure you, and if you pass out, the hospital is very close," Grandpa joked.

The kids got ready. They were very confused. Their grandparents were normally very nice, but was today's lesson about starvation? It seemed strange, but they decided they would go along with it and find out what this mystery was about.

When they all arrived at the grocery store, the lesson started at the fruits and vegetables.

Grandma began talking about demand and supply. She explained that it is usually called supply and demand, but she liked think about it the other way around.

Grandma said, "If there is no demand for something, there is no reason to supply it, because no one wants it. Or, if there is a supply, but no demand, no one will pay for it just because it is available. That is why I like to think about demand first, and then supply. Just like breakfast this morning; if your stomach said, 'I do not want breakfast,' then there would be no reason to supply a breakfast."

Grandma stopped at the grapes. "I like to have grapes all year round. But late in the summer, the price of grapes is cheaper than it is the rest of the year. Grapes are sometimes very expensive around Thanksgiving. My demand or desire for grapes is fairly steady year round, because I like grapes. But the price changes. What do you think causes the price to change?" she asked.

"Is it supply?" Kayla suggested.

"Yes, is it supply. There are many more grapes available in the summer. People get their fill of them and do not necessarily want to buy a whole lot more. So to move the grapes before they spoil, the price is lower in late summer," Grandma explained.

"I could eat that whole bundle of grapes myself," growled Ryan, still hungry from breakfast.

They saw a bread stand. The sign said, "$1.00 for one loaf, $1.80 for two loaves, and $2.50 for three loaves."

Grandma asked," Why do you think the price of the next loaf is less than the first?"

"Is it a demand thing?" Kayla asked.

"Yes, it is," said Grandma. "There is plenty of bread on the shelf. The supply is available. The theory of demand says a person is willing to pay more for the first of something and less and less as they get more of it. A person dying of thirst in the dessert would pay a lot more for the first glass of water than they would for the next and the next. They may not pay anything for glass number 100, as they could not drink or carry it."

"I feel like I am dying of hunger," Ryan pouted, pushing out his lower lip, tipping his head down, and shuffling his feet.

Grandpa jumped in and said, "We are going to take these groceries home and then we will go to the cafeteria for lunch. At the cafeteria, you can get a lot of food for a good price."

"Let's go before I pass out and have to go to the hospital!" joked Ryan.

After packing all the groceries away in the cupboards, they went to a very nice cafeteria and everyone loaded up on their favorite foods. They were all stuffed after eating too much.

Grandpa said, "So demand and supply determines the price. The price people want to pay and the price offered depend on how much people want something (demand) as well as how much is available (supply). So who wants to stop for a taco on the way home?"

"Are you kidding?" asked Ryan. "I am stuffed. My demanding stomach is happy right now."

"Yes, I was kidding," Grandpa replied. "I think you see your demand for a taco right now is low. So we are not going for a taco now, but we can another time. To make your money stretch further, you need to be aware that a trendy item or an item in short supply may cost more. Being aware of that makes you a better shopper and a better money manager. Demand is not just how much you want something, but how much everyone collectively wants something."

> Demand and supply determine prices. Trendy popular items will carry a higher price. Items in short supply will carry a higher price.

Grandma pulled out a Bible. She said, "One thing I want you to know is that the supply of eternal life is unlimited. Eternal life is free for all who have faith in Jesus, our Savior. Having faith is trusting in God's promises. Ephesians 2:8–9 says, 'For it is by grace you have been saved, through faith—and this is not from yourselves, it is the gift of God— not by works, so that no one can boast.' So the supply of eternal life is unlimited. God desires all to be saved as a free gift. The only problem is that too many people throw away eternal life by rejecting faith in Jesus. Remember lesson one about putting God first with your money: it is a Biblical way to strengthen your faith. Being aware of demand and supply will help you to be a better money manager. We want to use that knowledge to be fair and upright in our dealings with others. We do not want to be cheats. We will read Proverbs 11 tonight as devotion to learn more about being fair and upright in our dealings with others."

The kids appreciated having had a less active day. They wrote a note to their mom and dad and mailed it home. They checked out some of their favorite websites, listened to some music, and snooped around in some of Grandpa's old toys in the basement.

That evening, they read Proverbs 11 and learned more about what it means to be fair and upright. A worldly view is that "knowledge is power." But a God-pleasing view is that knowledge should be used to be fair and helpful to others and oneself.

Ryan stated, "I think I understand this demand and supply thing well enough that we can have more for breakfast than a few crackers. Is that okay?"

"Sure thing," Grandpa said. "Tomorrow is Saturday. I will fix pancakes and bacon, which I think is one of your favorites."

"Sounds good to me," replied Ryan. "What is the plan after breakfast?"

"We will let you know tomorrow," Grandpa said. "All our activities will all be at our house tomorrow."

The kids got ready for bed. They looked at some old comics they found in the closet and acted out a few of them for each other, hamming it up. Ryan acted out the water example from the day's lesson, pretending he was dying of thirst and drinking all he could from a big water bottle. They laughed at themselves for being silly and thought about how, even though they were having a good time, it would be good to head home in about a week.

CHAPTER 6

Time Value of Money

Saturday started more slowly than the previous days had, since they were planning to stay in the house all day.

About mid-morning, Grandpa led the children outside to the driveway to play a game. He said, "I have scattered a whole bunch of pennies in the driveway. We will call this the penny game. In this game, you will work together. The object of the game is to pick up all the pennies you can in two minutes. You can keep what you pick up, but you have to split the winnings."

"How many pennies did you scatter?" asked Ryan.

"About one thousand," Grandpa replied.

After a pause, Kayla exclaimed, "Wow, that is ten dollars!"

Down the driveway, they saw pennies scattered fairly evenly over a long distance. They could barely see the pennies at the far end.

Grandpa said, "You must gather the pennies and deposit them in this bowl at the starting line. You can only pick up pennies with your hands and you must hold them in your hands as you bring them back. Only the pennies in the bowl count. I will give you five minutes to decide on a strategy for how you want to play. You will have two minutes to pick up all the pennies you can. I have set up a clock so you can see the seconds counting down."

Ryan and Kayla discussed ideas. They decided they would make trips back and forth to the bowl, as they would not be able to hold many pennies at one time. They decided that someone would need to watch the clock. Ryan volunteered to glance at it from time to time. They peered out, looking at the pennies, trying to guess how many they could get. They also decided that Ryan would stay to the right and Kayla left so they would not bump into each other.

"Five minutes is up," Grandpa said. "Are you ready?"

"Yes, we are!" the kids said excitedly.

"On your mark, get set, go!" Grandpa chanted.

They picked up as many pennies as they could. Some bounced out of the bowl as they dropped them in. They became more frantic as they neared the end of the time.

"I think time is just about up. We'd better empty our hands quickly!" Ryan said. They almost fell over as they came running back.

"Bzzzz, time is up!" Grandpa said. "How about you go in and count your winnings? I think you got about one third of the pennies, so I would guess you picked up about 350, or $3.50. I will set up another game. But do not peek at what I am doing. I will call you when I am ready."

Ryan and Kayla went in and counted their pennies. Outside, Grandpa replaced most of the pennies they had picked up and added nickels further out, past where the pennies stopped.

"I'm ready!" he announced.

"We picked up $3.80!" said Kayla when they returned.

Grandpa explained the new game. "This game is almost the same as last one. I replaced the pennies so that there are a lot, just like last time, and I also added nickels further out, past where the pennies stop. I will give you five minutes to decide on a strategy. This time, pick up all you can—pennies or nickels—in two minutes."

"We want to do this game over and over and use quarters and half dollars!" Ryan exclaimed.

"I have not planned that, "chuckled Grandpa. "I am retired, you know, and I have to watch my nickels and dimes."

Ryan and Kayla strategized again. They figured it would take them extra time to run out for the nickels. In the first game, they had each made three trips to the bowl. They figured they could make at last two trips getting nickels, so it would be best to go for nickels first and watch the time.

"We are ready, Grandpa," Ryan said.

"You still have a minute to strategize, if you wish," Grandpa replied.

"We cannot wait. We are ready!" Kayla exclaimed.

"All right. Ready, set, go!" Grandpa cried.

They ran for the nickels first. The nickels filled up their hands fairly quickly. On their second trip to the bowl, Ryan said, winded, "I think only ten seconds left. We had better go for more pennies. There is not enough time to get to the nickels again, so get the pennies close by." They quickly grabbed some pennies and dropped them in the bowl. A brief moment later, Grandpa called time.

"Okay, go on in and count your winnings," he declared. "I will sweep up the leftover coins and we can talk about what we learned."

"Aw, no more money games?" Ryan moaned.

"I tell you what: If you sweep out the garage, you may keep all the coins left on the driveway," Grandpa offered.

"Sounds great!" the kids exclaimed.

Grandpa watched intently as they counted their winnings for round two. The total was $11.60.

"That is pretty good for two minutes of work," Grandpa said. "Tell me about your strategy."

The kids explained that when there were only pennies, they wanted to stay as close to the bowl as they could. When there were nickels further out, they were willing to go get them, instead. But when time was almost up in the nickel game, they went for the pennies that were closer. In both cases, they had had to be aware of the time, or else they might miss getting money into the bowl.

"Very good," Grandpa acknowledged. "You now understand the concept of the time value of money."

"We do?" Kayla asked, puzzled.

Grandpa explained, "The time value of money is a concept that having money now is preferable to getting the same money later. The closer pennies are like money now. If the money is all worth the same, you grab what is close. The nickels took more time as they were further away; they were worth the extra time to be gathered only because they were worth more. So let's think about managing money. If we delay getting money now, we will want more later for waiting. In other words, if I had a choice of money now and the same money later, I would choose to have the money now. If I had a choice of money now or more money later, I would want to know how long I had to wait and how much money I would receive later before I decided."

> Time value of money: A dollar today is more desirable than a dollar in the future, so if spending is delayed, the desire is to have more money to spend later.

"I have heard that a bird in the hand is worth two in the bush. Is time value of money kind of like that saying?" asked Kayla.

"Yes, very similar," Grandpa responded. "The future is uncertain. Two birds in the bush means that, later, you might have two in your hand, or one, or none. So a bird in your hand now is more valuable than two birds you may not be able to get in the future. Businesses make many decisions based on the concept of the time value of money."

Grandpa continued, "This time value of money is a key reason why lenders must charge interest for making a loan. If they give you money now, they want more money back later. So the person receiving a loan pays interest and the person giving the loan receives interest. Here is a useful Bible verse: Ecclesiastes11:1 says, 'Ship your grain across the sea; after many days you may receive a return.' This verse also talks about receiving a return. Would you rather have to pay interest to have money now, or receive interest and get more money later?"

"I would rather get interest for more money," stated Ryan.

"It really depends," Grandpa answered. "For example, if you borrow money for a business and that business can make more money than the cost of interest, you might be better off getting the loan to run the business and pay the interest. The key lesson here is that money now is more desired than the same money later. Earlier, we read and talked about the parable of the talents in Matthew 25. Recall that the servant with the least did not even put his money in the bank to gain interest. The others servants started businesses. The time value concept of money is not a new thing. We will expand on the concept of interest another day. How about you both clean the garage as we planned and then you can keep all the rest of the coins in the driveway? You get started and I will help in about an hour."

They had thought that cleaning the garage would take about ten minutes, so they wondered what Grandpa meant about coming out in an hour. But when they saw all the dust and junk in the garage, they were not sure they had made a good deal for the rest of the coins in the driveway. They thought it might take all day!

"How about one of us sweeps up the coins with the broom while I start moving stuff so we can sweep in the garage?" suggested Kayla.

"Sounds fine to me," Ryan replied.

They finished cleaning the garage in about three hours, with Grandpa's help. The grand total of the coins picked up was $22, or $11 each, and they were happy about their earnings. They finished the day watching TV, reading a few books, and daydreaming.

The next day was Sunday. There were no activities or games to learn about money this day. They went to church and Sunday school and learned that faith is trusting God's promises. The sermon was about how doubting God's promises is part of our sinful condition, but Jesus forgives us for our doubts, too. However, following God's plan and his will helps reduce our doubts and strengthens our faith so we do not fall away or reject his promise of eternal life with him. Later that day, they helped grandma plant some flowers and they visited a few of her friends.

CHAPTER 7

Compounding Is Key

At breakfast on Monday, Kayla stated, "This money stuff is more like a way of living than of just having a savings account. It must be like eating the right kinds of food to stay healthy."

"I think you are right," Grandma said, pondering. "Money is also a tool, kind of like the broom was a better tool for picking up coins than your hands were. Money is one tool to help you through life. Money can be used for good or, unfortunately, for bad. Like any other tool, if it is used in the proper way, money can do some great things."

"Ryan was using a tool the wrong way when he swatted me with the broom yesterday, before you came out. That was not the proper use of that tool!" Kayla exclaimed.

"Yes, it was!" Ryan retorted. "That was to get you back for kicking my dust pile at me."

"I think we are getting off track," Grandma interjected. "There is a saying: 'A fool and his money will soon be parted.' Do you want to know how money works like a tool?"

"Yes," Kayla replied.

"Let's get out the chess game and we will learn about compounding," Grandpa said.

The kids went to get the chess game. They had played a few times before, but they certainly did not remember compounding being part of the game.

Grandpa reviewed with them how the pieces moved and the rules of the game. They had a good feel for it and played a couple of quick games. As they were getting close to wrapping up, Ryan asked, "So, what about compounding? I do not think anything about compounding came up while we were playing chess."

"I wanted to get your brain warmed up," Grandpa replied. "This idea of compounding may be a little bit difficult. Are you warmed up now? How many squares are on the chess board?"

"Let's see, eight times eight is sixty-four," Kayla answered.

"Yes, eight squares in one row and eight rows," Grandpa replied. "Let's assume we put one penny on the first square in row one. Then let's double the number of pennies on each square as we go."

Grandpa showed them a table.

Square Number	Pennies	Dollar Value
1	1	$0.01
2	2	$0.02
3	4	$0.04
4	8	$0.08
5	16	$0.16
6	32	$0.32
7	64	$0.64
8	128	$1.28

Grandpa explained, "Notice how the number gets bigger faster. That is the idea of compounding. The numbers are building on themselves. If we continue this, make a guess of how much money might be on square 16."

"I will guess $50," said Kayla.

"I guess $40," said Ryan.

Grandpa showed them the next table.

Square Number	Pennies	Dollar Value
9	256	$2.56
10	512	$5.12
11	1.024	$10.24
12	2,048	$20.48
13	4,096	$40.96
14	8,192	$81.92
15	16,384	$163.84
16	32,768	$327.68

"In general, people are just like you. They underestimate the power of compounding. Square 16 would have a little over $327," Grandpa said. "As you can see, compounding grows quickly. If we kept compounding, on square 28 you would have over one million dollars. More precisely, $1,342,177. On square 44 you would have more money than the richest man in the world. It would be more than eighty seven billion ($87,000,000,000). I think you can see the point."

Ryan's eyes got big and he exclaimed, "Do we get to play this compounding game for real?"

"Yes, to some extent," Grandpa replied. "Remember the lesson about the time value of money? If we get money later, we want more money, not the same amount as today. So if we are to receive our money later, we want more money for having waited. Let us consider a bank that pays 3 percent interest. If you left $100 in the bank for one year, at the end of that year, you would have $103 ($100 x 1.03=$103). If you left the $103 in the bank for the year after that, you would have $106.09 ($103 x 1.03=$106.09). Notice that you make a little more than $3 the second year. At year three, you would have $109.27 ($106.09 x 1.03= $109.27). Can you see that you are gaining more than $3 per year because your money is compounding? It is compounding because your interest is making more interest. The money is a tool that works harder for you as it compounds. Here is a verse from the Bible about how it takes time to make money. Proverbs 13:11 says, 'Dishonest money dwindles away, but whoever gathers money little by little makes it grow.'"

"With the bank account example, how long do you think it will take for your $100 to double or grow to $200 at 3 percent interest?" Grandpa asked.

"Looks like it will take forever," Kayla said.

Grandpa smiled and replied, "There is a fairly simple way to figure the answer to that question. This is called the rule of 72. The rule of 72 works like this. Divide 72 by the interest rate; that is a close estimate to the number of years it takes to double your money. So in our example, take the number 72 and divide by 3, which is the interest rate. That will tell you the years it will take to double your money to $200. So, 72 divided by 3 is 24. In twenty-four years, at a 3 percent interest rate, you will have doubled your money to $200."

"Well, that certainly is not forever, but twenty-four years is a long time to me," Kayla piped up.

Compounding is key to long-term wealth.

- Compounding is increased with more time and higher returns.
- The rule of 72 is a good approximation of the time it will take to double your money. Divide 72 by the interest rate to estimate the years it will take to double your money.

"How about 10 percent—how many years will it take to double your money by compounding with a 10 percent return?" Grandpa asked.

"It must be a little over seven years?" Kayla suggested.

"Yes, a little over seven years," Grandpa replied. "Divide 72 by 10 to get 7.2."

Grandpa pulled out another table.

Type of Money Investment with All Returns Reinvested	Twenty-Year Average Return	Average Time to Double Money
Savings account	3%	24 years
Certificates of Deposit	4%	18 years
Company Bonds	6%	12 years
Large Company Stocks	10%	7.2 years

Grandpa pointed at the table and said, "So you can see that your money can make you more money by compounding. The higher the return rate, the faster you make money on your money and the sooner you will double your money. So, looking at this table, where would you like to put your money if you had some to invest?"

"I choose the 10 percent," Ryan exclaimed. "I like the idea of 10 percent better than 3 percent."

"I wish it were that simple," Grandpa replied. "The problem is that there is no guarantee for interest rates or returns over time. The better the guarantee of return, the lower the likely return rate. This is heading into another topic for later, called risk. We will learn more about risk in the next lesson. What I want you to remember from this lesson is that compounding happens when your money starts making more money on the returns, and also, that compounding is faster at higher interest or return rates. Time also makes compounding greater. If you remember the rule of 72, you can make quick estimates of how long it will take to double your money."

Grandma showed up. "How about today we go to the zoo?" she said. "They have some special exhibits and I heard they have some monkeys that play checkers."

They went to the zoo and had a great time seeing the various animals. They saw the monkeys that played checkers, but the checkers were actually big red and black throwing discs. All they did was throw them around. The monkeys were not as smart as the kids had thought they would be.

That night, as they got ready for bed, Ryan and Kayla contemplated.

"I think I need to go back to school and learn more about math so I will be a good manager of my money," Ryan whispered.

"Me, too," Kayla said. "Grandpa and Grandma really seem good with numbers. I wonder if they liked math in school. I guess school will be helpful someday. It just does not quite seem that way right now."

They said their prayers and practiced their multiplication tables to help them fall asleep faster.

CHAPTER 8

Risk and Reward

The children were a little apprehensive when they woke up, wondering whether it would be another day of crackers for breakfast. They were relieved to see a large selection of cereals on the table.

Kayla said, "Some of these things we are learning about money seem like they do not matter to us. We are just kids."

"Very true, but all learning is like that," Grandma responded. "You learn and then you apply. It is hard to apply something you have not learned. Just like in school, you learn so you can grow up to be a capable person. Here are two sayings I like. The first is, 'To grow old with dignity, you have to start early.' And the second is, 'You cannot have your bread and loaf too.' Do you get the loaf part? A loaf is an amount of bread and it also means being lazy. If you plant a garden, you start with seeds. So we are just planting a few seeds in your brains for now. Someday those seeds of learning will sprout some accomplishments."

"That explains why Ryan sometimes acts so corny. His head is full of corn seeds from eating those corn flakes," Kayla joked.

"Well I have already grown two ears from that corn—one on each side of my head!" Ryan joked back.

Grandpa said, "We will play a couple of games today to learn about risk. The lesson today is a difficult topic, I think the hardest one of these two weeks. Even if it does not all make sense to you now, I want you to be exposed to it so later on you will have heard about it before."

"Risk—I have played a game called that," Ryan commented.

Grandpa answered, "These games are about uncertainty, lack of understanding, and the chances of losing money."

"These games so far have been pretty fun, and we have made money each time," Kayla said.

"Let me explain the first game. You get to roll two dice. The rules are kind of complicated, so I have written them down for you," Grandpa said.

Dice game rules:

- Each of you will roll two dice each turn.
- You each will have up to thirty-six turns in one game.
- Before each turn, you must declare whether you are rolling for stocks or bonds, or if you pass. The terms *stocks* and *bonds* are only being used to get you used to those terms. They have no significant meaning in this game.
- If you choose to pass, you do not roll, but passing counts as a turn.
- You start you with $0.50.
- If you go broke, your game is over and you win nothing. If, after thirty-six turns, you have money left, you keep all the money.

- You must have at least $0.50 to roll for stocks, and $0.25 to roll for bonds.
- The table below shows your winnings and losses with each roll you declare.

	Declared Roll		
Roll Outcome	Stocks	Bonds	Pass
Double	Lose $0.50	Lose $0.20	Win $0.03
Two even numbers but not a double	Lose $0.25	Lose $0.15	Win $0.03
At least one odd number, but not a double, and the two numbers do not add up to 7	Win $.30	Win $0.20	Win $0.03
Two numbers add up to 7	Win $0.80	Win $0.25	Win $0.03

"This seems really complicated. We do not know how to win at this game," Kayla stated.

"Yes, it looks like the only thing we know is to take a pass every time," Ryan added.

"Very good observation," Grandpa said. "Risk includes not knowing what you are doing. Without more understanding of how to win, it looks like the only option we understand is a pass. That option has the lowest risk because it is most certain. You could say passing has no risk at all because the outcome is certain. We can, however, lower our risk or uncertainty by increasing our understanding. Let's look at a table of all the possible outcomes of rolling two dice."

Two-Dice Roll: All Possible Outcomes					
1,1	1,2	1,3	1,4	1,5	1,6
2,1	2,2	2,3	**2,4**	2,5	**2,6**
3,1	3,2	3,3	3,4	3,5	3,6
4,1	**4,2**	4,3	4,4	4,5	**4,6**
5,1	5,2	5,3	5,4	5,5	5,6
6,1	**6,2**	6,3	**6,4**	6,5	6,6

"We will study this together and I brought a calculator to help us figure some numbers," Grandpa said.

"If we start with $0.50 and take thirty-six passes, what will be our winnings?" Grandpa asked.

"Thirty six times $0.03 is $1.08. With our starting $0.50, that would be $1.58," Kayla answered.

"Correct, and that outcome is certain. No risk," Grandpa replied. "What could we make if we rolled for stocks, and every time, we rolled a number that added to 7? What would we win?"

"We would win 36 times $0.80 for $28.80, plus our original $0.50, for a total of $29.30," answered Ryan.

"Very good," Grandpa replied. "Do you think that is very likely to happen?"

"I do not think so," said Kayla.

"Let's assume we roll every possible combination one time. I have a table that shows the winnings if every roll was rolled one time for each strategy. I think if you study the table of all the outcomes, you can figure out how I came up with these answers. The numbers in parentheses are negative dollars, or losses," Grandpa said.

Roll every outcome one time	Number of Rolls and Winnings		
Roll Outcome	Stocks	Bonds	Pass
Double roll total rolls	6	6	
Lose $ Doubles	($3.00)	($1.20)	
Two even numbers but not a double total roll	6	6	
Lose $ two even numbers but not a double	($1.50)	($.90)	
At least one odd number, but not a double, and the dice do not add up to 7 total rolls	18	18	
Win $ at least one odd number, but not a double, and the dice do not add up to 7	$5.40	$3.60	
Dice add up to 7 total rolls	6	6	
Win $ dice add up to 7	$4.80	$1.50	
Number of passes if pass every time			36
Winnings total	$5.70	$3.00	$1.08
Grand Total winnings with starting $0.50	**$6.20**	**$3.50**	**$1.58**

After they reviewed the table, Grandpa said, "If you played this game many times, only rolling for stocks, and you never went broke, it appears that on average, you would win $6.20. But if the game is played only rolling for stocks every roll, in several of those games, you would go broke early on. Actually, in one game out of six, you would be broke on the first roll. Do you see how I came up with that? You could also go broke after several rolls. So knowing the average outcome is a very difficult question. Going broke is not a good thing; you lose your starting $0.50 as well. If you play the game many times, only rolling for bonds, it appears you would win $3.50 on average, but you also could go broke rolling for bonds. However, when rolling for bonds, you would need three bad rolls in a row to go broke. So going broke with bonds is not very likely."

"I still like the idea of rolling for stocks every time," Kayla stated. "However, like you said, if you start the game rolling for stocks and your very first roll is a double, you would be broke and the game would be over."

"Great observation," Grandpa said. "Even though right from the start you have enough money to roll for stocks, you have a 6 in 36, or 1 out of 6 chance, to lose all your money on the first roll. A better strategy would be to roll for bonds for a couple of rolls to have a cushion built up before you start rolling for stocks, because there is too much risk of going broke if you roll for stocks too early. On the other hand, rolling for stocks may give you higher winnings. Even though your knowledge of this game has reduced your risk of playing it, there is still uncertainty. Where there is uncertainty, there is risk. Are you ready to play?"

"Yes, let's do this," the kids replied.

At the conclusion of the game, Ryan had $9.90 and Kayla had $3.05.

"If you share some of your observations of the game, I will give both of you $10 instead of your winnings," Grandpa said.

"Thank goodness," Kayla replied. "I rolled for bonds on my first five rolls to make sure I did not go broke. Ryan only rolled for bonds on the first roll. At the completion of roll 9, I was actually

$0.05 ahead of Ryan. Later on, I lost $1.50 in three straight rolls for stocks. Because of my fear of losing a lot at the end, my last four rolls were for bonds. That was a very good decision because I had some bad rolls at the end."

Ryan said, "I just got really lucky. I rolled for bonds one time and stocks the rest of the way. At one point, I got two 7s in a row, which added $1.60. I rolled for stocks at the end because I had quite a lot of extra money built up. That was a good decision because I was lucky again and had all winning rolls at the conclusion."

"Interesting," Grandpa said. "You both had the same knowledge going into the game, yet you both made opposite decisions in the end. Can you help explain that?"

"Ryan did not have several losers in a row like I did. That bad string of losses made me hurt, and I even thought of taking a pass or two," Kayla said. "If Ryan had experienced some bad losses, he would not have been as risky rolling for stocks at the end of the game."

"Very good observations from both of you," Grandpa replied. "This game was much like the real world. Chance can result in large differences in outcome. However, understanding can help you manage your chances better. Did you notice that both of you did much better than taking passes the entire game? So even though there was risk and uncertainty, taking a risk had a better payoff than the certain outcome of taking all passes. I have another game for you to play outside."

They put the dice away, Grandpa gave them each $10, and then they went out the door to play the next game.

Grandpa had two piles of balls set out in the yard. One pile was tennis balls and one pile was ping-pong balls. About forty feet away was a long stick that Grandpa called the target line. The line was laid out left to right. He explained, "Kayla gets to throw tennis balls and

Ryan ping-pong balls. The object of the game is to see how close you can get your balls to the line." They each took ten practice throws.

"This is not fair," said Ryan. "These ping-pong balls are harder to throw well."

"Don't worry," said Grandpa. "It will work out in the end. Let's start the game. Each of you now gets to throw twenty-four balls as close to the line as you can. It is only the distance in front of and behind the line that matters; do not worry about the distance to either side. Take your time and do as well as you can."

They threw twenty-four balls each. Grandpa had them count out the sixteen closest tennis balls on either side of the line. He put down two yellow strings to mark the range where these closest sixteen tennis balls had landed. That left eight balls outside of the yellow strings. One yellow string was closer to the throwing position and the second yellow string was further past the line. Then they counted out the closest sixteen ping-pong balls and put down two white lines, as they had for the tennis balls. The white lines were further apart than the yellow ones since the ping-pong balls had been harder to throw accurately. Then they picked up all the rest of the remaining balls.

Grandpa further explained, "We will call the area between the two yellow lines the range for Kayla. The area between the two white lines is the range for Ryan. The range of the tennis balls is shorter than the range of the ping-pong balls. Do you see that? The range for the ping-pong balls is longer because they are harder to throw accurately. This time, when we throw the balls, I will give you $1 for every ball you get inside your range, but for every ball that lands outside your range, I will take away $2. We will play three games in total of twenty-four throws each. So you will be throwing a total of seventy-two balls. Since this is just a game, if your grand total after three games is less than zero, you will not owe me anything.

When you throw, you should still try to hit the original target line, but for sure try to land your balls inside your range."

"So can I throw the tennis balls now?" asked Ryan.

"No, sorry, you throw the same balls as before," Grandpa stated.

The kids were thinking that this game was even better than the dice game. They could make $72 each. All they had to do was throw all their balls between their two lines. They started throwing and Grandpa scored every throw. The detail of each throw is captured in the table for game one. The scoring summaries of games 2 and 3 and the grand total score are shown as well in the following tables.

Game 1							
	Ryan				Kayla		
Throw	Too short	In Range	Too long	Win-nings running total	Too short	In Range	Too long	Win-nings running total
1	1			-$2		1		$1
2		1		-$1		1		$2
3	1			-$3		1		$3
4			1	-$5		1		$4
5	1			-$7		1		$5
6			1	-$9		1		$6
7		1		-$8		1		$7
8		1		-$7		1		$8
9		1		-$6		1		$9
10		1		-$5		1		$10
11		1		-$4		1		$11
12		1		-$3	1			$9
13		1		-$2			1	$7

	Too short	In Range	Too long	Winnings	Too short	In Range	Too long	Winnings
14		1		-$1		1		$8
15	1			-$3	1			$6
16		1		-$2			1	$4
17		1		-$1		1		$5
18		1		$0		1		$6
19		1		$1			1	$4
20		1		$2	1			$2
21		1		$3			1	$0
22		1		$4		1		$1
23			1	$2		1		$2
24			1	$0			1	$0
Total	**4**	**16**	**4**	**$0**	**3**	**16**	**5**	**$0**

Game 2 Summary								
	Ryan				Kayla			
Throws	Too short	In Range	Too long	Win‑nings	Too short	In Range	Too long	Win‑nings
Total	**5**	**17**	**2**	**$3**	**4**	**17**	**3**	**$3**

Game 3 Summary								
	Ryan				Kayla			
Throws	Too short	In Range	Too long	Win‑nings	Too short	In Range	Too long	Win‑nings
Total	**3**	**16**	**5**	**$0**	**4**	**16**	**4**	**$0**

Grand Total Three Games								
	Ryan				Kayla			
Throws	Too short	In Range	Too long	Win‑nings	Too short	In Range	Too long	Win‑nings
Total	**12**	**49**	**11**	**$3**	**11**	**49**	**12**	**$3**

"Are you a little surprised about how this turned out? You each won $3. Did you think you would have done better?" Grandpa asked.

"If I had quit in the middle of game one, I would have been better off," Kayla said as she studied the numbers. "The bad streaks reminded me of the bad streaks in the dice game."

"I started off terrible," Ryan explained. "But I got better, or lucky, and it turned out okay. Before the game, I thought I would make at least $50. But it looks like Grandpa knew something ahead of time. Still, I am happy with three dollars."

"Risk is related to the certainty of the outcome," Grandpa explained. "If the outcome is certain, there is no risk. I know you were trying to land the balls inside the range, but no matter how hard you tried, some were either long or short. In applying risk to money, your confidence of the outcome plays into your decision of risking money. If the outcome is not certain, there is risk. I was risking my money in this game, but I had some understanding of how often you would likely land the balls in your range. With money, the higher the risk, the less confident you can be, so the reward has to be higher to make taking the risk worth it. I know this is a rather abstract topic, but think about it for a while."

"So how did you know that we would not win a lot of money at this game?" asked Kayla.

Grandpa explained, "I was pretty confident you would land about 2/3 of your throws into your range. Let me explain how I guessed that. You will hear several new words you may never have heard before, so hang in there with me for a while. There is a math concept called normal distribution. Normal distribution is a set of events or measurements that tend to hover around an average, or target, just like the balls you threw at your target line. These data points can be plotted on a graph or curve, and sometimes this is called a bell curve. If we average the distance of all the balls from your target line, the average will very likely be near the target line. So this game had a normal distribution around your target line. Both of you had the same target and the same average throw.

"There is another term called standard deviation. For a normal distribution, a range of one standard deviation will capture about 68 percent of the events, or about 2/3 of the events, inside the range of one standard deviation. The distance between each of your range lines was one standard deviation because it captured 2/3 of your trial throws. Even though you each had the same average or target, you had a different range or standard deviation. The ping-pong balls, being harder to throw accurately, had a wider range. I was rather confident your future throws in general would land inside the range of one standard deviation, about 2 out of 3 times, so the balls would land outside the range about 1 out of 3 times. Giving you $1 for landing in the range and subtracting $2 for being out of it was a calculated bet on my part that your total winnings would balance out fairly close to zero. So as a review question, how many events are outside the range of one standard deviation?"

"I think you said 1/3 or one out of three, would be outside the range because 2/3 are inside," said Ryan.

"Correct. Here is a harder question: About how many events would be below the range?" Grandpa asked. "That is closer to where you threw the balls."

There was a long pause while they continued to think. Kayla said, "One half of 1/3 as a fraction is 1/6. So I think one out of six will be below the range and one out of six will be above the range."

"You are right, Kayla," Grandpa said proudly. "With this knowledge, you already know more about statistics than most people do. If you see something about range or standard deviation, you know right away there are a variety of outcomes to consider. The average is good information, but that alone does not tell you enough. There will be many outcomes on either side of the average. You now know that one standard deviation will capture about 2/3 of the likely events. About 1/6 will be below the range of one standard deviation and about 1/6 will be above the range. The average is the target, or central point where the data or events hover around."

Grandpa pulled out this table and explained some more. He said he would explain stocks and bonds further over the next few days. For now, he wanted them to focus on average returns and the standard deviation.

Type of money investment	Twenty-year average return	Average time to double money	Standard deviation of the last twenty years of returns
Savings account	3 percent	24 years	Plus or minus 0.5 percent
Company bonds	6 percent	12 years	Plus or minus 4.0 percent
Large company stocks with dividends reinvested	10 percent	7.2 years	Plus or minus 15.0 percent

Grandpa said, "Throwing tennis balls was kind of like the company bonds line. The range of standard deviation was less because the tennis balls were easier to throw more accurately. The range for ping-pong balls was kind of like the stocks line, with a wider range, so a wider standard deviation."

He also explained this table had some made-up numbers, but that the numbers were fairly realistic to the last twenty years and that the higher the standard deviation is, the higher the risk. He explained that if you want your money back in one year, the savings account is less risky because you can be quite confident you will get your money back with at least some interest in one year. However, based on the past, if you want your money back in one year, with large company stocks, you really do not know where you may be in a year. He said the only thing you can know for sure is that, over the last twenty years, large company stocks have returned 10 percent on average, one year in six it likely had a negative return of 5 percent or worse, and one year in six likely had a return of 25 percent or more. The standard deviation for stocks had a range wider than bonds. Also, who knows what the future may be? He compared this to Ryan's first game throwing balls. In game one, Ryan was behind for some time, but he caught back up in future throws.

As far as real money goes, Grandpa explained that if you have just a few years, a savings account is best because you do not want to risk a loss. However, if you have three to seven years, large company bonds might be a good choice because they have a better interest rate than a savings account, but also a medium degree of risk. If you have at least seven or more years, large company stocks may be the better choice. He did not want to complicate the illustration, but he mentioned that there are many more options for saving and investing. He cautioned that the future is not known. These averages and standard deviations are past results, and may not repeat in the future; you cannot be certain that what has happened in the past will happen again. He suggested that Kayla probably thought, in the middle of her first game of ball toss, that she was going to get a lot of money from the game. But as the games progressed, the final results were closer to the average.

Grandpa said, "Taking out a loan to invest in stocks or bonds would be extremely risky. Your investment could lose money and you would have to repay the loan, as well."

Risk includes

- Not knowing what you are doing
- Uncertain outcomes
- The chance of losing money

Historically, over long periods, the higher the risk, the higher the reward.

Risk is described mathematically by standard deviation of the past results.

One standard deviation is the range that captures about 2/3 of the past results. About 1/6 of the data is lower and 1/6 is higher than one standard deviation.

Grandpa concluded, "So, when money people or financial people talk about risk, they are mostly talking about standard deviation of past results. They use math to calculate standard deviation from the past and use that number as a measurement of risk. The higher the standard deviation, the higher the risk. Risk is not only the chance of losing all or part of your money, but also the possibility to make more. People who take low risk or no risk over long periods of time typically miss much of the power of compounding because of lower return rates. To capture the power of compounding, you need time and a higher interest rate. But getting higher interest rates requires accepting more risk. A person should not take higher risk unless they do not need their money back for many years. I know this is a little beyond you right now, but you will have relevant experiences sooner than you think, and this learning will be of benefit to you."

"I was thinking my arm hurts from throwing those balls, but I think my head hurts even worse," said Kayla.

"I agree," said Ryan. "Grandpa, do you think you can help me with my money someday, when I actually have some?"

"Yes, I would be happy to," Grandpa answered sympathetically. "This lesson on risk is the hardest. It is a few years ahead of you, but it is good for you to hear about it now."

"There is another aspect of risk. Here is another famous saying: 'Do not put all your eggs in one basket.' In terms of money, do not put all your money in one place. That one place may go broke, or have a disaster. Diversifying is putting your money in more than one place so that your chances of losing all your money are lower. Ecclesiastes 11:1–2 has something to say about diversifying. It says, 'Ship your grain across the sea; after many days you may receive a return. Invest in seven ventures, yes, in eight; you do not know what disaster may come upon the land.' The power of compounding helps your money work for you. Compounding is helped by time and higher return rates. Return rates, on average, are helped by assuming some risk, but to avoid a possible disaster, you need to also diversify. All of these concepts boil down to knowing what you are doing."

They felt the first few drops of rain. The drops turned into a full rain storm so they quickly went inside.

"The weather man said there was a 50 percent chance of rain today. It is raining now, so you can see that weather forecasting is also about uncertain outcomes," Grandpa said. "On another topic, insurance is a way to safeguard against financial loss from serious events. I would be remiss if I did not mention insurance as a way to cover some unforeseen risks in life. But insurance is one topic we can visit in a few years."

They stayed inside the rest of the day. They played checkers, chess, and Scrabble, taking a few breaks to eat. Then they helped with the dishes and gathered up all the trash.

That night after prayers, Ryan asked Kayla, "What was that Bible verse about a fool and his money?"

Kayla contemplated this and said, "It was not a Bible verse. Grandma said it was a famous saying. 'A fool and his money will soon be parted.'"

"Grandpa was not a fool today," Ryan responded. "He knew we were not going to make a lot of money at that ball toss. Also, he seems to have money, so he must not be a fool—otherwise his money would be gone. I think I need to pay more attention in school studying these subjects so I am not a fool with my money."

"You are fooling around," Kayla groaned. "You think about money too much. That will make you a fool, too."

"I guess you are right. Listen to the rap I thought up: 'Money's just a tool. A tool not for a fool. A tool that makes us drool. Compounding is astounding. Demand and supply. Risk and reward. Money makes us more ... of who we are already. So if I am a fool ... more money just makes me a bigger fool.'"

"Now you are really losing it. Remember, a fool does not get more money; he parts with his money. Go to sleep before you turn into a fool. Now I cannot get your foolish rap beat out of my head. Good night," Kayla groaned.

"Goodnight," Ryan whispered, yawning.

CHAPTER 9

Every Benefit Has a Cost

By the time Wednesday came, the grandchildren were wondering if they would finish the lessons on money before their mom and dad come to get them on the weekend. They had a conversation about it at breakfast.

"Are we going to finish our money camp by Saturday?" Kayla asked.

"Yes, counting today, we have three more lessons," Grandma said.

"I kind of like this money camp we are having. I am making quite a lot of money at it. I am glad I brought my cool bank," Ryan replied with excitement. "So what is the plan today?"

"We are going bicycle riding on the trail that follows the river. We have our two bicycles, and the neighbors said we could borrow two of theirs," Grandma explained.

"Sounds great, but what about the money? Are we going to make some more today?" Ryan asked enthusiastically.

"No money to make today. Learning is just as important as making money. We will explain more during our bicycle ride," Grandma replied.

They gathered up the equipment, checked the tires, and packed a picnic lunch. The river was not too far away. There was a nice paved bicycle trail to follow which crossed roads by diving under bridges. The path had places to cross the river and three beautiful parks.

They stopped at the highest point, where they could see the busy activity of the city. Grandpa said, "See that factory over there? We own a piece of that."

"You bought Kayla and me a piece of that factory?" Ryan said with excitement.

Grandpa replied, "No—by we, I mean your grandmother and me. We also own a piece of that fancy large hotel, that railroad, and that store. We have some money loaned to that company off in the distance. We have a piece of many more companies outside our state and a few in other countries."

"Wow, you must be a lot richer than I thought," Kayla said dreamily. "How do you own a piece of so many companies?"

Grandpa explained, "A company can be owned by one person— that is called a sole ownership. If two or more people own the company, that is a partnership. A company can also be owned by many people, where each one owns a piece of the company. These owned pieces are called shares, or stock. As the owner of a share, you can receive some of the company's profits. The profits from stock shares are called dividends. Dividends are a portion of the money left after all costs or expenses are paid. That leftover money is called profit."

Grandma said, "Let us consider a lemonade stand. If you sold $15 in lemonade and the sugar and lemons you used to make it cost $8, the profit would be $7. Profits are the money left after costs. In our lemonade example, if seven people owned the stand, each owner would profit $1 for their share."

Grandpa said, "A company can take out a loan by selling bonds. So, bonds are one type of loan. You can loan money to a company by buying one of their bonds. Bonds pay an interest rate that does not change. Loans are a cost to the company, not a profit, and they are obligated to pay the interest whether they make money or not. The company could go broke, however, and not be able to pay. People who buy bonds are paid interest on the bond for loaning the money. If the company has trouble and needs more money to keep the business running, bond holders are better protected than stock owners because the stock owner's dividends are paid last. Stock owners only share profit if the business makes a profit. But if profits are good, stock owners are paid best. As a company grows, the value or price of a company share can go up. However, bond values do not change much with company growth. So while stocks have more risk of loss, they also can have more reward."

Grandpa talked about the stock market. He said, "The farmers' market is where fruits and vegetables are sold. The stock market is simply the store where stocks and bonds are bought and sold. Stock and bonds can be purchased through a broker, or you can buy shares in a mutual fund, where money is collected from many people and the fund buys shares from many companies and tracks your pieces specifically for you."

"Most of our invested money is in mutual funds," Grandpa said as he wrapped up. "I checked yesterday and, based on our account, we have about $1,500 in that factory and about $2,000 in that hotel. So we do not have as much as you think, but it is spread around well. We have a little of so many things that our money works for us, and that is how we are providing for ourselves in retirement. The money lesson for today is that every benefit has a cost. To have the benefit of our money working for us, we had to invest it rather than spend it. But now, because of those investments, we have that money and more to spend."

> Business benefits have a cost. The benefit of compounding returns or sharing business profits comes at the cost of investing your money and reinvesting the returns rather than spending it.

Grandma said, "When it comes to money, you have four basic choices. Those four choices are to give, save, spend, or invest. Giving is giving to God's ministry or to another person, as we learned in lesson one. Saving is keeping your money to spend later at a future date. This is money you do not want to risk because you want to "bank" on it being there when you want or need it. Saving is like putting your money in a savings account. Spending is trading your money for something you need or want. In this case, the money is gone. This is like the money you spend on a movie, food, clothes, and the like. Finally, there is investing. When you invest your money, you hope to get more back later from the investment. The benefit of more money later comes at the cost of investing it and the time it takes to see returns."

"Let's work a simple example of an investment," Grandma said. "Let's assume your dad decides to buy a bicycle in order to save money. In total, it costs about 50 cents per mile to drive a car. Let us assume that riding a bicycle costs nothing per mile to ride. Your dad does some shopping and sees that a good bicycle that is comfortable to ride costs $500. So, the benefit of free miles has the cost of $500 for the bicycle. He also assumes he will ride an average of about 500 miles per year. Here is a question: What are his benefits and what are his costs?"

Ryan and Kayla came up with the following.

Benefits
- Free miles on a bicycle
- Get exercise riding the bicycle
- Bicycle could be used for fun rides

Costs
- $500 for a bicycle
- Takes longer to get places on a bicycle
- Need a place to store the bicycle
- Fixing flats and other items to take care of the bicycle

"Great job on your lists," Grandpa said proudly. "Let us focus on the money aspects of considering the purchase of the bicycle. Payback period is a fancy term used to mean the time from when you invest your money to when you get the same amount of money back. So how many years of riding a bicycle would it take for your dad to get back the $500 he invested on a bicycle?"

Ryan and Kayla discussed it and presented the answer: two years. They explained that he had to ride 1,000 miles, saving $0.50 per mile, to have $500. Since he planned to ride 500 miles per year, it would take two years because he was saving $250 per year.

"Correct answer," Grandpa replied, smiling. "Now how long from when he buys the bicycle until he doubles his original $500, or has $1,000 of returns?"

Ryan and Kyla discussed it again and answered four years, because $250 per year for four years is $1,000.

"Another correct answer," Grandpa replied, smiling and raising his eyebrows. "Now what was the interest rate he got on his investment in the bicycle?"

Ryan and Kayla talked about it and then Kayla replied, "We do not have a clue."

"I think you can figure it out," Grandpa explained. "Remember the rule of 72? It says to divide 72 by the interest rate to get the time it takes to double your money. If you know the time to double your money, divide 72 by the years to double and that will be the interest rate. In the bicycle example, it takes four years to double the money. After two years, he would get his money back, and after four years, he would double his money. So if you divide 72 by 4, you get 18 percent by using the rule of 72. That is a pretty good return rate on the investment. Then your dad could spend the extra money he saved by riding his bicycle, but to get the benefit of compounding, he would need to invest the money he saved in something else, like he did with his bicycle investment. Remember, compounding is when the money you earn makes more money. To make money in a business or investment, you must invest your money rather than spending it. That is your cost. If you invest wisely and have enough time for compounding to help you out, hopefully you receive your money back and more."

"You can see that the investment of $500 in a bicycle could result in more money later," Grandma said. "The cost is the investment of $500 in a bicycle, and four years of riding it could result in getting double the money back. It will take time to know for sure. So there is a risk; getting more money back later may not happen."

"Let's think about gifts for a moment," Grandma continued. "Gifts are not free. All gifts come at a cost, too. The cost of the gift was taken care of by the giver, so even gifts have a cost. The receiver is the person who gets the gift without a cost. If there is a cost to the receiver, then it is no longer a gift. Let's think about putting God first. Eternal life is a free gift to us because Jesus paid the price for us. That gift is something to be thankful for forever. He must love us a lot to give us a gift like that for free."

"So remember, in the business of money, all benefits come with a cost," Grandpa summarized. "Let's ride further and then eat lunch. After that we can decide how much more we want to ride this afternoon."

They ate lunch and rode along the bridge across the river. The fresh air was wonderful. They talked about how the modern world works and how amazing it is that it works as well as it does. They discussed how learning about managing money today is as important as growing your own garden food was 100 years ago. They notice a man who appeared to be living under one of the bridges and wondered what had happened in his life, or whether that was the life he had chosen to live. Ryan and Kayla and their grandparents were all very thankful for their family and their situation.

Before bed, Grandpa called Ryan and Kayla to the computer and showed them the current prices for shares of some of the companies they had seen that day. He explained a little more about dividends. He also showed them a few stock and bond mutual funds and how much money they had made over the years. The earnings varied a lot—some years were losers.

After prayers that night, Ryan pondered aloud, "In school, we learn vocabulary words, but I do not remember ever coming across words like the ones we learned today—stock, bond, payback period, dividend, and interest. Those would make a good vocabulary lesson in school! The way Grandpa explained them kind of makes sense.

But to really understand them, you need the words and the math. It does not make sense without the numbers, either."

"Yes," Kayla replied as she pondered. "I am realizing it takes language and math to be a good money manager."

Ryan said, "We have been talking about constructing money principles. I can see how you could dig a lot more with a machine than with a shovel. You could probably make more money, too, but you would have to invest money to buy the machine first, and then you would need money to fill it with fuel. It sure would be fun to buy a big digging machine."

"I like planting flowers," Kayla replied. "So I would be just fine digging with a shovel."

They were thankful to have a loving family and a nice place to sleep that night.

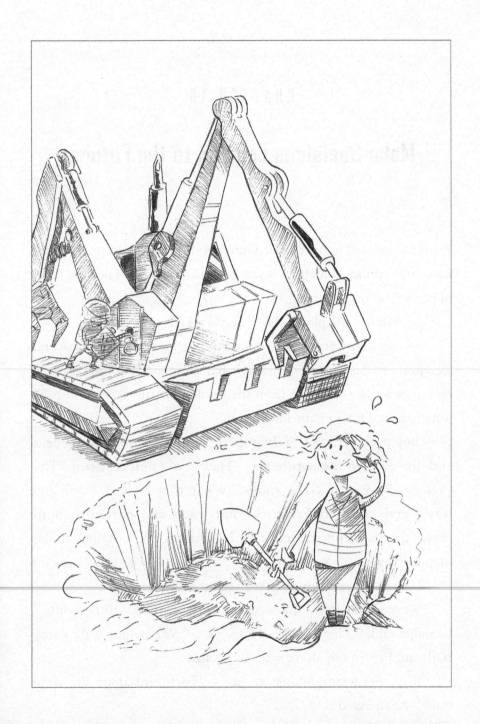

CHAPTER 10

Make Decisions Looking to the Future

Breakfast seemed to have settled into a routine. There were no more feasts and no more crackers. Ryan was glad to have his normal bowl of cereal and orange juice.

"So, what is the plan today?" Kayla asked.

Grandma answered, "Today we go for a hike. There is a natural area just a few miles out of town. It has some nice big hills, woods, and streams. We have not been there for some time. We will pack some chicken for a picnic lunch, too."

They packed up lunch, bug spray, sunglasses, and hiking gear and drove off to the nature area. They saw a sign that said "The Preserve for Future Generations." When they arrived, Ryan and Kayla grabbed their backpacks and water and started to head down the path, but Grandpa and Grandma were stalled at the map display.

"Let's go, I am ready to hike!" Ryan exclaimed.

"We need to study this map to see where we will be going," Grandpa said. "This is quite a large place. We cannot walk every trail, and I definitely don't want to get lost."

"If we get lost, couldn't we just go backward along the same trail?" Ryan asked.

"I suppose we could. But that would be a waste of our fun time; I would rather spend a few minutes looking at this map," answered Grandpa as he finished making some notes.

They went down the trail. Very soon there was no sign of the parking lot or trail head. All they heard were the sounds of the wind whistling through the trees and birds chirping.

"Where are we going?" asked Kayla.

"Based on our plan, about a mile ahead we can see a waterfall from the bottom. Then we will have lunch down by the river, where there are some nice sandbars. If you wish, later, we can walk up along a short cliff and see the top of the waterfall. After that, we can go back to the car or, if we have enough energy, walk up to an observation tower. Does that sound okay?"

"Sounds great to me! I am glad you made a plan by studying that map," Kayla responded as she skipped ahead.

There were many interesting trees and plants. They saw a dozen different birds and heard even more. The kids noticed Grandpa was taking notes again.

"Grandpa, what are you doing taking more notes?" Kayla asked.

"I am taking notes on how often either of you looks to the side or behind you and what happens when you do," Grandpa replied.

"What? Why would you be doing that?" Kayla asked, puzzled.

"I will tell you the first time I see you looking back after the waterfall," Grandpa said.

They arrived at the waterfall and stopped to enjoy the bubbling noise, cool air, and calm it provided. There were several rocks to climb and a few low tree limbs which provided a nice challenge for climbing. After a refreshing break, they started walking again. After going just a little way, Ryan and Kayla both stopped and glanced back at the waterfall.

"That's it!" Grandpa squawked like a bird.

"That's what?" asked Ryan.

"You looked back," Grandpa stated. "Now before I give you my observations, walk twenty steps further down the trail while looking back behind your shoulder."

Cautiously, the kids took twenty steps forward while looking back over their shoulders. Luckily, the path was fairly wide and level. Then Grandpa said, "Here are my observations. You tended to look back when there was something interesting behind you. When you did look backward earlier on the trail, you stood still and did not try to walk. You seemed to take in more detail when you looked backward than when you were walking forward. Now tell me about your effort to walk forward while looking backward over your shoulder. What was that like?"

Kayla said, "I was not very good at it. I did not know where I was going. I concentrated a lot on each step, but not much about where I might be going. I did get to see the waterfall for longer, and I enjoyed that."

Ryan added, "Same here. I was counting each step because I wanted to get it over with. Walking and looking forward is much better."

"Here are some more observations," Grandpa continued. "When we stopped at the map, we were not moving anywhere. But those few minutes resulted in a future plan. When you looked back, you stopped and focused in on a few details you wanted to remember. I noted also that when you walked while looking back, you walked very slowly and very cautiously. That is the money lesson for today."

"What? That is the money lesson?" Ryan mumbled. "These lessons seem to be riddles."

Grandpa answered, "You are right, Ryan. "These lessons are like riddles. Doing something like hiking comes naturally. Common sense is what you learn by doing things. So as we hike along, we are learning the common sense of hiking. Common sense is not quite as easy when it comes to money."

> Financial plans and decisions are better made looking to the future. What happened in the past is helpful to know, but you must plan and act looking forward, not backward.

He went on to explain how stopping at the map to plan the hike is like making a plan with our money. When we look back to the past of what happened with our money (both in spending and investing), we pick up a few details and remember them. Those memories can help future plans, but the key is to put a plan into action. If you are stuck and only study the plan, or dwell on what happened before, you will never move forward. As with hiking, spending all day looking at the map means you will not hike. But spending no time at the map means the hike will likely not be as fun. A good plan considers the future and what it may be like. A bad plan only dwells on the past. Dwelling on the past too much is like walking while looking back behind you. You will not progress very quickly and you will be very cautious. And yet, if you never look back, you will not remember important events.

Grandpa wrapped up and said, "The penny and nickel games were also an example of thinking and planning for the future. You thought about what was best for the penny game and changed your plans for the nickel game."

Grandma said, "The problem with the future is that no one knows it." She pulled out the following Bible verses.

> Since no one knows the future, who can tell someone else what is to come?
>
> —Ecclesiastes 8:7

> [Jesus:] "Suppose one of you wants to build a tower. Won't you first sit down and estimate the cost to see if you have enough money to complete it? For if you lay the foundation and are not able to finish it, everyone who sees it will ridicule you, saying, 'This person began to build and wasn't able to finish.'"
>
> —Luke 14:28–30

Grandma said, "In terms of money, the future is unknowable, but that does not mean we should not plan. If you have a plan, then as the future happens, it is easier to make adjustments— just like walking forward is easier than walking while looking backward. There is one certain thing in our future, as Jesus said in Mark 16:16: 'Whoever believes and is baptized will be saved, but whoever does not believe will be condemned.' So whatever our plan for our life, we certainly do not want to lose our faith in Jesus, our Lord and Savior. That would be a bad future. A good future is one with Jesus and starts with the plan of including him in what we do now."

She continued, "Here is one more Bible verse from Matthew 6:19–21. Jesus says, 'Do not store up for yourselves treasures on earth, where moths and vermin destroy, and where thieves break in and steal. But store up for yourselves treasures in heaven, where moths and vermin do not destroy, and where thieves do not break in and steal. For where your treasure is, there your heart will be also.' Jesus is not saying a plan is a bad thing; he is saying that we should be thinking and planning our ultimate future of eternal life with him. That is far more important than anything on earth."

They spied the river just ahead. "I sure am glad we planned lunch," Ryan said. "I would not want to die and enter eternity on an empty stomach!"

"Well, at least you are thinking about your future," Grandpa quipped. "We have made some poor decisions with our money in the past. But we learned from them and moved on. We also made some very good decisions. We learned from those good decisions, too, and we continue to learn. As far as money goes, if you dwell on your failures, you are doomed to failure. If you dwell on your past successes, you may not have future success. In all cases, learn from the past, but look to the future when making decisions."

They finished lunch and enjoyed the river view. They walked the cliff to see the waterfall again, then they went to the tower and decided they had just enough energy to climb it. They arrived back at the car in the late afternoon. On the way home, they took off their shoes and rested their feet.

That night, before they all got ready for bed, Grandpa said, "You know, the future is a bit scary. It is unknown to us. But we are not to worry about the future. Neither should we be reckless about it. Pastor Tom tells us, 'I do not know what the future holds, but I know who holds the future.' We know that, too. Jesus holds our future. Faith is trusting God's promises. And he said he would care for us."

Grandpa said, "I have a special prize for whoever can race upstairs, put on their pajamas, and be back here first. On your mark, get set, go!"

The kids tore out of the room and scrambled to find their pajamas. Kayla knew exactly where she had placed hers. Ryan lost time looking for his. In what seemed like a blink of an eye, Kayla raced back. Ryan tried to save face and ran as fast as he could, but still showed up second.

"Kayla, your prize for coming in first is $5! And Ryan, your prize for not giving up is $5!" Grandpa announced. "Life is like that; it is more about not giving up than how fast you are."

Grandpa read Hebrews 12:1–3. "'Therefore, since we are surrounded by such a great cloud of witnesses, let us throw off everything that hinders and the sin that so easily entangles. And let us run with perseverance the race marked out for us, fixing our eyes on Jesus, the pioneer and perfecter of faith. For the joy set before him he endured the cross, scorning its shame, and sat down at the right hand of the throne of God. Consider him who endured such opposition from sinners, so that you will not grow weary and lose heart.'"

Grandma said, "Everyone's future on earth is different. But our ultimate future can be the same: eternal life. Keep that in mind as you grow up and have to make difficult choices—not only about what you will do with your money, but also about what you put into your mind, your mouth, your ears, and your life."

"Good night," Grandpa and Grandma said.

The kids went off to get ready for bed. "I am thinking about that lesson on planning," Kayla said. "If you are building a house, it is not enough just to have a house plan. You need to think about whether the plan fits your lot. You need to think about how you are going to use your house in the future because you will be living there. Likely, there will be some things in your present house that you want to copy, but also you will want to change some things or add new ones."

Ryan was fixated on counting his money. "Five more dollars," Ryan told Kayla. "I am going to remember that lesson on not giving up."

"I do not think you were listening to me. Let me tell you this: I got $5, too, and I also got the pleasure of beating you!" Kayla said. "Winning can be fun, but I understand it is not all about winning. It is about doing your best. Only one more money lesson to go. I cannot imagine about what it might be about."

"I have no idea either," Ryan replied.

They finished their prayers and, tired from their long hike, quickly fell asleep.

CHAPTER 11

Destiny

It was Friday morning and the grandchildren met Grandma and Grandpa at the kitchen door on their way to breakfast.

"Today is our last day of money camp," Grandma announced.

"Albert Einstein was famous for his mental experiments," Grandpa said. "Today we will do our money lesson as a mental exercise without an object lesson. We will use just our minds. Then to celebrate finishing your summer money camp on the nitty-gritty of money, we will go to the amusement park for the rest of the day. Sound okay?"

"Awesome!" Ryan and Kayla responded.

Grandpa pulled out a piece of paper with the following written on it.

- Sow a thought, reap an act
- Sow an act, reap a habit
- Sow a habit, reap a character
- Sow a character, reap a destiny

"Do you know what sow and reap mean?" he asked.

"To sow is like to farm or plant, like grandma does her flowers," Kayla said.

"To reap is like to harvest or to get your reward," Ryan answered. "We learned those terms in Sunday School."

Grandpa said, "There is some debate about whether thoughts come before actions or actions come before thoughts. I read a quote once that said, 'Hard work can only accomplish what the mind has first envisioned.' I believe thoughts come before actions most of the time. Anyway, the key point I want to make is that, on earth, people seem to strive for five Ps. Those five Ps are power, prestige, pleasure, popularity, and possessions. Which of those do you think is money?"

"I would say possessions," Kayla answered.

"I agree, but it could also be power, I suppose," Ryan offered.

Grandpa said, "I think you've got the idea. Money may be a significant part of all of those Ps. If people's thoughts center on themselves, then their actions and habits will center on themselves, too. Their character will be self-centered like the five Ps can be self-centered. So, no matter what their possessions, power, prestige, pleasure, or popularity, other people will see that they have a flawed character if those Ps are used primarily in self-serving ways. Even if they appear to do charitable things, people will wonder if they are trustworthy. If a person is self-serving in all their pursuits, then when they die, you have to wonder what will happen to them. On the other hand, people can use those same five Ps as a way to reflect their love for Jesus in ways that are not self-serving."

He continued, "To put it more simply, people are defined by their character, not by how much or little money they have. Character cannot be purchased, and your character should never be sold. Character is more valuable than money. Character is the essence of who you are. Our ultimate destiny will come after we die. On earth, we need to focus on our character."

"So why did you spend all this time teaching us about money?" Ryan asked.

"The lessons were not all about money. They were also about thoughts, actions, and habits of good character," Grandpa explained.

"What makes a good character and a good destiny?" asked Kayla.

Grandpa explained that our thoughts should begin with Jesus in mind. "Put him first. With our money comes a tithe. We do not just think and pray about tithing; we do it. If we weave God into our life and money, everything will work out. Our character will become more of one who shows love for his Savior and who loves his neighbor as himself. Let me read you Matthew 22:37–40 'Jesus replied: "'Love the Lord your God with all your heart and with all your soul and with all your mind.' This is the first and greatest commandment. And the second is like it: 'Love your neighbor as yourself.' All the Law and the Prophets hang on these two commandments."' In these four verses Jesus spelled out pretty clearly what character he desires from us."

Grandpa added, "Jesus explained that it is okay to love ourselves. However, we should love God first and we should not love ourselves more than our neighbor. Jesus does not want those five Ps of power, prestige, pleasure, popularity, and possessions to separate us from him, and he does not want them to separate us from our neighbors, either."

Grandma said, "Jesus talked about building a house on a rock. The house with the solid footing stood through wind and rain because it was built on solid ground. Character that is, like the house, built on solid ground will be fine. But the house without a good foundation failed. You can read about it in Matthew 7:24–27 and Luke 6:46–49."

Grandpa shared some more Bible verses.

Whoever loves money never has enough; whoever loves wealth is never satisfied with their income. This too is meaningless.

—Ecclesiastes 5:10

[Jesus:] "No one can serve two masters. Either you will hate the one and love the other, or you will be devoted to the one and despise the other. You cannot serve both God and money."

—Matthew 6:24

Peter answered: "May your money perish with you, because you thought you could buy the gift of God with money!"

—Acts 8:20

Therefore, holy brothers and sisters, who share in the heavenly calling, fix your thoughts on Jesus, whom we acknowledge as our apostle and high priest.

—Hebrews 3:1

For God so loved the world that he gave his one and only Son, that whoever believes in him shall not perish but have eternal life.

—John 3:16

"I did not realize there was so much about money in the Bible," Ryan stated.

Grandpa replied, "Money is something that easily gets in the way of our thoughts. When money is too much on our thoughts, we can get distracted and forget the love God has for us. Our thoughts should be based on our faith in Jesus, and our actions and habits should be an outgrowth of those thoughts as a reflection of the love Jesus has for us. Our earthly character should show the fruit of the Spirit which is love, joy, peace, patience, kindness, goodness, faithfulness, gentleness, and self-control. If we keep our faith, our destiny will be eternal life with Jesus. Remember, faith is trusting God's promises. Our destiny of eternal life with Jesus is not because of our actions or efforts, but because of faith in what Jesus did for us."

Grandma added, "Following the path Jesus desires for us does not mean life will necessarily be easy. On the contrary, it may be harder, we may be persecuted, and people may make fun of us. But we can rest assured of the gift of eternal life in heaven. So if our money follows us on this path, we will be good managers with our money and fair in our money dealings. We must manage money with intelligence and diligence. Recall that being diligent is being careful and persevering in work. On this path, our money can magnify our character and be an even better mirror of Jesus, our Savior. So we are finishing our lessons on money where we started. We finish with our thoughts and our destiny with Jesus, our Savior."

> You are defined by your character, not by your possessions, power, prestige, pleasure, or popularity.

"Are you going to teach this in Bible class?" Kayla asked. "This sounds a lot like a church lesson."

"Maybe," Grandma replied. "I hope the experiences of the last two weeks showed you, with actions, about money from a Christian point of view."

"I think they did," Ryan replied. "Are we going to the amusement park soon?"

At the amusement park, they rode several thrilling roller coasters, attended a magic and dance show, and ate hot dogs, ice cream, and more. It was a great day. It was a carefree day. It was a day to enjoy and to have a good time. The children noticed how Grandpa and Grandma interacted with people of all kinds in a caring and considerate way. They noticed how thankful they were to have the money to provide Ryan and Kayla a day at the amusement park. They really had seemed to grow old with dignity.

After prayers that evening, the children talked about their mom and dad arriving the next day. They were sure their parents would want to know what they had done over the last two weeks. But they were not sure they could remember everything.

CHAPTER 12

Conclusion

Saturday, Ryan and Kayla ate breakfast late. They were putting away the dishes and cleaning up when they saw the family car pull in. They raced outside to greet their parents with hugs, and then the four of them slowly made their way back into the house.

Dad asked, "So what did you learn this couple of weeks?"

"We learned to put God first with a tithe of our money," Kayla proudly answered. Then there was a long pause. "And ..."

"And something like compounding is astounding," Ryan said.

"And something about mean teachers, I mean something about living and means," Kayla fumbled. "I am afraid this is hopeless. I don't seem to be able to remember much of anything. And I do not know what to do next with some of my money."

"I have forgotten it all, too," Ryan confessed.

Grandpa came to the rescue and said, "I know this was a lot of information and it was hard to remember, so I wrote down all our activities and lessons for you in this book. Now you can read about yourselves and be better with the nitty-gritty of money."

"Yes, the nitty-gritty of money, that is what we learned," Ryan said. "But we still do not know what we should do now, since we do not have much money."

"We have a plan for you," Dad stated. "You learned some money principles these last two weeks. Let's put them into practice. Let's take 10 percent and give it to God's ministry. Of the money remaining, you can spend half; half will go into your savings account. As you earn more money from your allowance, we can do the same. So we will give 10 percent to church, then save and spend the remainder in equal parts. Also, Grandpa and Grandma were generous and gave each of you a starting investment account. This account is called a custodial account because your mom and I are also on it. Until you are eighteen years old, you have to have an adult or custodian on the account with you as a helper. You are a few years away from eighteen. Until then, we can do some observing and learning about how investing and business work. Also, this will give you some firsthand experience of some of the money lessons you've had over the last couple of weeks. With this plan, you will practice what you have learned in regards to giving, saving, spending, and investing."

> Start being a money manager now. Start with a simple plan and grow with it. Give, save, spend, and invest.

"Does my investment account own a piece of that factory we saw the other day?" asked Ryan.

"It could if we purchase some shares of the company, or a mutual fund that will purchase those shares," Dad explained.

"You know, I actually half know what we are talking about," Kayla said. "Two weeks ago, it would have sounded like gibberish. By the way, is nitty-gritty gibberish, or does it mean something?"

"Nitty-gritty is a slang word,' Grandma explained. "Nitty-gritty is more fun to say than boring basics. So rather than say we learned the boring basics of money we can say that we learned the nitty-gritty of money. But after you know some of the basics, or nitty-gritty, of managing your money, it can be rather fun and not boring at all."

"Yes, it feels like we have constructed some money principles which we can practice," Kayla said.

"Kayla and I have been constructing pictures in our minds about what we learned. It feels like we have some drawings or sketches to get us started,' Ryan added.

"We would like to play some of the games and do some of the activities again when we get home. Do you think we can do that, Mom and Dad?" Kayla asked.

"Sure," Mom replied. "I think we may even be able to come up with a few more."

They all spent several hours talking about the adventures they had had and the games they had played over the last two weeks. Grandpa told some stories of the games he played with their dad and his sister when they had been growing up. The kids explained that it had been a fun couple of weeks learning about money, and they definitely liked the money they had earned.

As they exchanged their good-bye hugs in the driveway, Grandma said, "Here is a note for you to read when you get home. See you soon and don't forget all the nitty-gritty of what Jesus did for us!

After they arrived home they all sat at the table. Mom said to Kayla, "How about we eat a few pieces of that candy you made. While we have our treat would you read the note from Grandpa and Grandma?"

"Okay," Kayla said. "It says, 'Dear Ryan and Kayla, We sure enjoyed your stay and hope you learned about money from a Christian perspective. We learned a lot from you too. Your excitement and outlook on life is refreshing to us older folks. We are really proud of you and your family. We welcome you anytime and hope to get to your house soon too. We have three more Bible verses which we would like you to read. These are all quotes from Jesus which are found in three different Gospels, so he must have thought this to be important. We would like for you to pass the verses around and read them individually to yourself. After you read them have a family discussion of what you think Jesus is telling us in these verses. You may want to look up and read a few verses before and after these verses as well. Love, Grandpa and Grandma.'"

> What good will it be for someone to gain the whole
> world, yet forfeit their soul? Or what can anyone give
> in exchange for their soul?
>
> —Matthew 16:26

> What good is it for someone to gain the whole world,
> yet forfeit their soul?
>
> —Mark 8:36

> What good is it for someone to gain the whole world,
> and yet lose or forfeit their very self?
>
> —Luke 9:25

APPENDIX

Nitty-Gritty Principles of Money

1) With all things, put God first. A tithe (10 percent) is a good benchmark for putting God first with our money.
2) Be content: Know the difference between wants and needs.

   - Live within your means.
   - Avoid debt in daily living.
   - Practice saving.

3) More money just makes you more of what you already are, so learn and practice your money values early on.
4) Budgeting is setting and following priorities and choices about money and time.
5) Demand and supply determine prices. Trendy, popular items will carry a higher price. Items in short supply will carry a higher price.
6) Time value of money: A dollar today is more desirable than a dollar in the future, so if spending is delayed, the desire is to have more money to spend later.

7) Compounding is key to long-term wealth.

- Compounding is increased with more time and higher returns.
- The rule of 72 is a good approximation of the time it will take to double your money. Divide 72 by the interest rate to estimate the years it will take to double your money.

8) Risk includes

- not knowing what you are doing,
- uncertain outcomes, and
- the chance of losing money.

Historically, over long time periods, the higher the risk, the higher the reward.

Risk is described mathematically by standard deviation of the past results.

One standard deviation is the range that captures about 2/3 of the past results. About 1/6 of the data is lower and 1/6 is higher than one standard deviation.

9) Business benefits have a cost. The benefit of compounding returns or sharing business profits comes at the cost of investing your money and reinvesting the returns rather than spending it.

10) Financial plans and decisions are better made looking to the future. What happened in the past is helpful to know, but you must plan and act looking forward, not backward.

11) You are defined by your character, not by your possessions, power, prestige, pleasure, or popularity.

12) Start being a money manager now. Start with a simple plan and grow with it. Give, save, spend, and invest.

Printed in the United States
By Bookmasters